WINTER LOVE SONG

MEREDITH KINGSTON

THORNDIKE
CHIVERS

This Large Print edition is published by Thorndike Press®, Waterville, Maine USA and by BBC Audiobooks, Ltd, Bath, England.

Published in 2003 in the U.S. by arrangement with Maureen Moran Agency.

Published in 2003 in the U.K. by arrangement with the author.

U.S. Hardcover 0-7862-5993-0 (Paperback)
U.K. Hardcover 0-7540-7743-8 (Chivers Large Print)
U.K. Softcover 0-7540-7744-6 (Camden Large Print)

The text of this Large Print edition is unabridged.
Other aspects of the book may vary from the original edition.

Set in 16 pt. Plantin.

Printed in the United States on permanent paper.

British Library Cataloguing-in-Publication Data available

Library of Congress Cataloging-in-Publication Data

Kingston, Meredith.
    Winter love song / Meredith Kingston.
        p. cm.
    ISBN 0-7862-5993-0 (lg. print : sc : alk. paper)
    1. Skiers — Fiction. 2. Ski resorts — Fiction.
    3. First loves — Fiction. 4. Divorced women — Fiction.
    5. Sun Valley (Idaho) — Fiction. 6. Large type books.
    I. Title.
PS3561.I53W56 2003
    813'.54—dc22   2003056744

WINTER
LOVE SONG

CHAPTER ONE

"Single!"

Felicia looked ahead of her in line and noticed the young man waving his ski pole in the air. Then he shouted again, "Single!"

"Single, right here," she called back to him, and she began to maneuver her skis around the couples waiting in front of her. No one seemed to mind that she was moving forward in line, for it was a common custom when waiting for the double chair lift to allow lone skiers to group into pairs.

"That's what's so great about being a single," the young man chortled to everyone nearby as Felicia slid toward him, pushing her skis expertly through the deep grooves that had been worked into the snow by those ahead of her on the chairs all morning. "You meet the most interesting people."

Some of the other skiers embarrassed Felicia by sneaking looks at her rosy face, which was colored by the cold of the morning as well as the unexpected focus of attention the young man had placed upon her.

Smiles of agreement greeted his next loud comment as Felicia took her place beside him. "Look what I got for myself. Just about the prettiest blonde skiing at Sun Valley today, I'll bet."

Felicia lowered her voice to the point where it was barely audible against the sounds of the diesel lift engines nearby. She hoped to hint to her newly acquired companion that their conversation needn't be shared by everyone in the lift line.

"My name is Felicia Hollingsworth. Thanks for moving me ahead in the line. I'm a little late getting onto the slopes this morning, and I'm anxious to get started."

"The name's Joe Posten, best hot dog skier in the state of Idaho," he said. "Now here's the important question. I asked for a single; you'd better just be single."

Again he was speaking more to the group of people around them than to her, so Felicia ignored his question, concentrating instead on the couple ahead of them who had just stepped into position for their chairs. Felicia knew that she and Joe would be next, and, mercifully, whatever conversation she had to share with him would soon be held in the privacy of midair.

She watched the empty chairs come down the lift from the top, make the turn just behind her, and then move across the ramp to scoop up the waiting skiers for the trip uphill. Then she expertly sidestepped herself into waiting position for the next chair, feeling the surge of excitement that she always felt just before starting up the mountain for a day of skiing. She switched both ski poles to her outside hand and turned her head slightly to spot the chair's approach. Then she felt that reassuring pat on the fanny as the chair bumped her into it, and her heavy legs, supporting boots and skis, swung up into the air under her, and her effortless flight up the mountain was begun.

"I can't figure you out," Joe suddenly blurted out as soon as they were airborne. Their chair was carrying them over the narrow and almost-frozen Wood River.

"What can't you figure out?" she asked.

"I'm trying to decide if you're a bunny or not. Everything you're wearing is brand new, just like a first-timer. But you handle those skis like you've been on them before."

"I've done a lot of skiing."

"Then how come all the new duds? You're wearing the new women's racing boots that cost a bundle. You a rich girl or something?"

"Hardly!" Felicia laughed. "If I had to buy my own ski clothes, I'd be skiing in blue jeans. These are all new products I'm trying out. I work in a ski shop."

"All right!" He drew the words out for emphasis. "My kind of woman, I can see that. I've put in some hours in a ski shop in Boise. We got a lot in common."

Felicia took a deep breath, pushed out her lower lip, and directed a burst of air upward across her face so that it lifted her long blond bangs off of her eyebrows momentarily. If Joe had known her better, he would have paid heed to this warning gesture. Though she appeared complacent, and she had a long fuse, when her redoubtable temper finally exploded, her annoyer was usually bowled over.

"Say, as long as we're getting to know each other so well, are you finally going to answer that question of mine about being single? You aren't wearing a ring or anything."

"My, you are observant," she said, slipping her leather gloves back on.

"You got to be when you're picking up chicks. Got to look for all those clues."

"Hey, look," Felicia said, planning some strategy. "We're at the top of the River Run already. You going to ski here or go on up?"

"What are you going to do?"

"I asked you first," Felicia said, sitting up straight and preparing to get off of the chair lift. She planned to get eager young Joe committed to some plan of action so that she could do anything different to get away from him, or else she suspected she'd have his ski tips coming up on her the rest of the day.

She knew she should learn to be more friendly to such young men. She could almost hear the envious voice of her friend Nadine back home, laughing and telling her to loosen up and enjoy life, and take advantage of the men who were attracted to her clean outdoor look. Actually Joe was probably about her own age, and if she could view him impartially, she would have to judge him attractive. But she hadn't come to Sun Valley to meet men — in fact she was probably one of the only young women who hadn't — so the sooner she steered Joe toward more promising companions, the better.

As they neared the crest of a hill the snowy ground rose up to meet them, and in a moment their skis met the earth once more, and they were stepping out of their chairs.

"You say you've done some skiing. Let's

11

see how good you are," Joe challenged. "Let's schuss down River Run as fast as we can, and scare all the beginners to death."

"Lead the way."

Felicia forced an ambivalent smile to her face, and then smiled with real relief when she saw Joe dig his poles in, push himself forward, and start toward the top of the easy run without turning around to check on her progress. He was too anxious to show off his prowess on skis to consider the fact that she might not be following him. She quickly stepped off in the opposite direction, skiing toward the next chair lift that would take her on up to more challenging bowls.

On the next leg of her journey her companion was an older man wearing black boots with laces and baggy wool ski pants that dated him. He was in as contemplative a mood as she was, preferring to whistle tonelessly between his teeth as he took in the scenery below them rather than indulge in meaningless prattle. Now Felicia at last had time to examine her surroundings. As she looked down between her dangling skis, she remembered every run and cat track she was seeing beneath her. After so many years they were still as familiar to her as the streets near her own apartment in Los Angeles.

"You been to Sun Valley before?" her seatmate asked her quietly, as if he were shy about interrupting her thoughts.

"This is where I first learned to ski. I came here with my mother when I was a little girl."

She hadn't come near Mount Baldy on that trip, for she was a beginner skier and her lessons were confined to the Dollar and Half Dollar slopes nearer the lodge. Each afternoon she would excitedly run to find her mother who was usually lounging by the heated outdoor swimming pool in a new bathing suit. Felicia would tell her mother all about what she'd learned that day, and then they would plan their evening, for her mother had found that a ski resort offered a lot of social life, even for the nonskier, and she was a woman who appreciated fun and good times.

Years later Felicia had returned to Sun Valley, this time as a ski team member and a contender for a spot on the Olympic squad. Day after day she had tested herself on Mount Baldy's steepest slopes, watching her stern coach, trying to emulate his perfect form. Sometimes it was almost dark by the time she let her skis cool off on the gentle inclines of River Run that slowed her down on the way to the parking lot and the buses waiting to transport the last hearty group of skiers back to the village. How young and full of life she had been in those days, the warm currents of competition and optimism coursing through her, giving her vitality.

The man beside her turned to look at her with a start, for she had let out an admiring "Ooooo" and a gasp as she'd caught sight of a figure skiing below her with the strength and courage she'd always worked to achieve. Seeing the object of her awe, her seat partner began watching too, and soon both of them were absorbed as they watched a figure in black flying across the hazardous steep crests of snow, always in total control and as graceful as a dark bird in a wintery white sky.

"Boy, can that man ski!" the man beside her said, almost to himself.

"Yes, look at everyone else standing at the sides watching. It's usually hard to impress the skiers on Exhibition."

Felicia drew in her breath again, admiring the aggressive attack the man was making upon that minefield of moguls that was known as Exhibition Run. She looked down on the breathtaking drop, studying every contour of its pebbly face. The moguls, produced by the actions of large numbers of skiers taking the same routes down the hill, grew every season into huge proportions, particularly where the traffic was heavy, the snow soft, and the hill the steepest. The use of the new shorter skis had made the bumps sheer-sided, like trenches, and even more challenging when approached at the mounting high speed of this young racer.

"I wish I could believe that I will ski like that someday," the man grumbled. "They say practice makes perfect, but I've been practicing for twenty years, and I know I'll never be able to take Exhibition like that."

Felicia had skied it time after time, racing downhill to try to pare a few seconds off the course at some point or another. Sometimes she'd followed her coach, sometimes he followed her. But always she had skied with his vision in her eye, trying to copy him and attain his speed.

"There was a time when I could . . . ," Felicia began. But then she cut off the words with a toss of her straight, long hair. She didn't like to think about the past. The only way she could deal with the present was to see it as an entity in space quite separate from whatever led up to it. There was only the present and maybe the future to consider; there was nothing to be gained

15

from a study of her past.

Soon their chair passed over the skier on Exhibition, and the man beside her began preparing to get off the chair at the Round House, but Felicia turned around in her seat to gaze downhill at the disturbing figure that was racing out of her sight, hidden now by a forest of pines at the edge of the run. When she could see him no longer, she still had a vivid image of him in her mind. It seemed as if she had watched him before. She felt as if she could sense at what point he would shift his weight to begin his step turn, how much flex he would put into his knees as he approached a particularly forbidding mogul, how far into the hill he would lean as the pitch of the slope increased. She felt as if she could ski behind him like a shadow, imitating his form, and staying in his trail exactly, instinctively.

And his black parka, black pants, and black ski cap were so unusual, and yet so painfully familiar. Grant had always worn black. Even in those days few people had worn all black every day that they skied. But Grant always had. He said black was a warmer color. And he said his team could study his form better in black against the white of the snow.

Nowadays both men and women skied in

clothes colored like the rainbow. In fact the bibbed overalls that Felicia was wearing were yellow, and her yellow jacket had an actual rainbow design appliquéd across the front and back, with curving stripes of red, green, purple, and blue.

"There's the Round House," the man next to her said to draw her attention to the fact that it was almost time to alight from their perch. "Boy, a cup of coffee will taste good right now."

"I haven't even had my first run, yet," she laughed, "and you're already talking about a coffee break."

"You going to start right out with Exhibition?" he asked her as a joke as they stepped off the chairs and let themselves slide down the ramp toward a big open space below the mountainside restaurant.

Felicia was pulling her tinted goggles into place, for her light blue eyes were extremely sensitive to the glare of sun on snow. "I haven't been on skis since last season, so I think I'll warm up a bit on Lower College, first. Good luck with that coffee. No spills, now!" she called to him.

Felicia's muscles seemed to purr to her with pleasure, so happy were they to be stretched and pushed again, and given a chance to show how strongly they could support her skiing. Her style had always been smooth and easy, and through the years it had changed very little. She'd probably lost a lot of her speed and daring, but those had never come easy to her. What came to her quite naturally was the gliding downhill motion that made her seem to be floating when she was actually moving much faster than everyone around her.

Now as she eased her way across the broad bowl of Lower College, she kept her eyes almost closed so she wouldn't see the terrain as her boards rapidly approached it. Instead she let the soles of her boots tell her everything she needed to know when it was time to react. No anticipation was necessary. She was barely winded when she got to the cat track at the bottom of College.

Feeling very confident after her warm-up run, she skied toward the lift line faster than she normally would, indulging in a showy parallel stop that sprayed snow several feet into the air. She was immediately sorry to have called attention to herself, for she heard a familiar voice call to her from the chair that was just pulling upward over her head on the swinging cables.

"Felicia, baby. Sorry I lost you. Where will I meet you?"

Felicia cupped her hands around her

18

mouth and called out, trying to match Joe Posten's loud tones, "Top of the mountain," biting her lower lip then at her deceit, knowing full well that she planned to get off again at the Round House midway up the mountain and take on her old challenge, Exhibition Run.

A few skiers were straggling toward the chair lift, but there was no line, so within a few seconds she was back on the chair, ready to be whisked up the hill again. This time the seat beside her was vacant, and she enjoyed the solitude by looking around her in all directions, even turning in her chair to stare across the wild Sawtooth Range of the Rocky Mountains and toward the broad, flat plain where the town of Ketchum, Idaho, was visible beyond the parking lot.

Her eyes were drawn to a smudge of black two chairs behind her, and she craned her neck to see around the two teen-agers swinging in the air immediately following her. It was a man, and he was wearing black, but it was impossible to tell if the man was the one she'd seen skiing earlier. He was just too far away. But she had the strange feeling that an intense stare had been coming toward her from that direction.

This time she skied right off the chair lift and past the restaurant to the very lip of Exhibition without stopping. Then she paused to take in the shattering effect of the drop before her. She stood feeling the same nervousness that had always gripped her before every race. She felt the tug of the tendon in the calf of her left leg, almost as if it was demanding her attention, reminding her of the time she'd fallen, hurting it so painfully.

She knew that several skiers had paused behind her, waiting for her to step over the edge and begin her descent down the almost-vertical slope. She was hearing the voice of the starter at the beginning of a race, as she bounced into her crouch position just before beginning her downhill plunge. "Ten, nine, eight, seven . . ." She had hated that pressure then, and she hated it now. And yet she loved sports and knew that a competitor doesn't improve without constant testing, pushing, trying harder.

"Follow me," she heard a harsh voice say loudly near her left shoulder. Just then a dark figure shot past her over the edge of the precipice, and at the sound of the commanding words she pressed her ski poles down hard, bent her knees, and leaned forward to propel herself right into his fantail of spraying snow, directly behind him and down the treacherous face of Exhibition.

This was the part of skiing she liked, no more time for thinking, just feeling: hearing her skis chatter across the hard-packed snow that seemed like a bumpy sidewalk, feeling the sting of snow as it bit into her face as she turned abruptly into her own wake, feeling the upward thrust of her knees toward her chest as they jolted her over a nasty bump, absorbing the shock. There was no time to wonder who had ordered her to start this mad race, or why she had been so instantly obedient.

The figure ahead of her was setting a good pace, but she was able to keep up with him. It was just like following Grant in the old days. When his long body swayed, hers did too. And where he chose to make his turn, she made an identical turn a split second later. Their bodies were similarly built, both long and lean, with strong arms and legs that seemed to assist in their propulsion.

Halfway down he took a mogul straight on and shot into the air two or three feet before landing. Felicia was ready for it and coasted off its sloping side. Felicia was learning from him. She was watching his mistakes, and she was copying his moments

21

of pure form. Grant was teaching her again, and she was loving every minute of it. Grant could show her how to make it fun; Grant could invent new ways to make her body respond. With Grant to follow she knew she was doing her best. She hadn't had so much fun skiing in years.

She was sorry it was all over so soon. The wild crescendo of speed and crazy turns and startling bumps suddenly quieted as the hill leveled out. The man in black was snaking himself sensuously down the center of a mildly sloping ravine in a slow, easy *wedeln* that drew discouraged moans of admiration from the learning skiers struggling to cross it at safe right angles. Felicia's breath was still coming in frosty quick clouds of excitement, so she slowed down, pulling her goggles off her face to hang about her neck, and tossing her long hair out of her eyes as she worked her way down the middle of the bowl.

She had let herself believe she was skiing with Grant again. For just a few minutes she had enjoyed reliving a time in her past that she rarely let herself recall: those thrilling days when Grant Mitchell was coach of the women's U.S. team and Felicia was battling for a permanent spot on the downhill racing team. In those days Grant had skied with her every day, and then spent every minute of his off-duty hours with her as well.

At the bottom of the hill the man in black had come to a stop and was leaning his angular frame against his ski poles, his head turned away from Felicia. He had taken off the cap and was running his hands through his thick hair, but it appeared he still had the cap on, for his hair was just as black as the cap had been. How strange to encounter a man so similar to Grant, here of all places, she thought. She was certain he couldn't be Grant, for she had heard he spent most of his time in Europe now, and besides, it had been five years since she'd seen him, and he certainly must have changed more than this identical remembrance of him she'd conjured up to ski with.

"Felicia, you still ski as beautifully as ever," he said, turning toward her suddenly when she pulled up to a stop beside him. He spoke with an inflection so casual that he might have been continuing a conversation of five years ago.

Her pulse responded with an out-of-control staccato beat as it furiously pumped blood to her brain in an effort to resuscitate her thinking processes. She froze with a stunned look as she realized she had responded to him quite automatically, feeling the familiar force of his male magnetism before she'd known for sure who he was.

"Grant, it is you!" she struggled to say, her voice sounding young and breathless in spite of her efforts to seem undisturbed. "How did you know it was me?"

The dark eyes which had been studying her now flared into bright life. "I recognized your voice the minute I heard you calling out to that lovesick calf on the chair lift. I thought you were giving him one of your outrageous lies, so I followed you just to see if I was right." He looked down into her eyes, now unprotected by the tinted lenses and squinting under the harsh glare of the day and his look. "I've always had trouble telling for sure when you're lying and when you're telling the truth."

"What a terrible thing to say!" She bowed her head so that her thick honey-colored lashes veiled her eyes.

"This is the first chance I've had to tell you what I think about what you did. Can you blame me for wanting to get something off my chest?" he said as one black eyebrow lifted to mock her discomfort.

Felicia bundled her jacket about herself,

suddenly feeling chilled to the bone by the flashes of remembrance that he had sent reverberating through her brain. She had felt wrenching sorrow before their final parting, she had experienced a pain which ever since she had tried to block from her mind. Why did he have to reappear so suddenly in her life and bring those unhappy days back to her? She stared up at him, her brow furrowed with the unspoken question.

"You certainly don't seem happy to see me," he said, rolling up his knitted cap and zipping it into a pocket of his parka.

"Should I be?" she snapped.

"Come on, you look cold just standing there," he said from between firm straight lips that she knew all too well. "Let's get in that lift line and go on up to the Round House." He poled away from her with his usual arrogant assumption that she'd do whatever he ordered.

On the flat surface he was moving like a cross-country skier, using the strength of each long leg and opposing arm to pull himself along. She could almost see the power surge through his massive leg muscles beneath the taut fabric of his black nylon ski pants. Obviously he had kept himself in perfect shape, for he still had that economy of movement of a practiced athlete, that well-tuned body that could always be counted on to perform for him exactly as he wanted.

As she moved into his track to follow him, she was still reeling from the disquieting effects of this reunion which she had so long avoided. There was a thrill mixed with real dread at being again in his dynamic presence.

She had come here on vacation, a vacation she badly needed. She had hoped to find solitude, and time to work out her problems and make decisions about the future. She certainly hadn't come to Sun Valley with any thoughts of encountering Grant Mitchell. Her ex-husband was about the last man in the world she wanted to run into at this point in her life. He was stirring uncomfortable old passions within her, feelings that had long been put to rest and were best forgotten. She breathed a deep sigh of resignation, and a calming breath for courage, and followed him toward the lift line.

CHAPTER TWO

As Felicia and Grant made their way toward the lift line, she was conscious of the envious looks all the girls were giving her for having such a captivating partner to ski with. They couldn't know how she hated being with him, what hurts she was subjecting herself to.

They stood in strained silence. There was nothing they could say to each other which they would want anyone to overhear. They had once been married, but it had been a short marriage, and it had been a long time ago. Much had happened to both of them since. And now each stood quietly beside the other, reviewing those intervening years thoughtfully.

When at last they were alone together, suspended in the slowly progressing chair over a fairyland scene of snow-brushed pine trees and whorls of drifted snow, Felicia could feel Grant staring at her.

"You haven't changed a bit," he said finally, his voice husky with that unique grating quality to it that she remembered so well.

"Oh, I'm sure there have been a lot of changes in five years."

"No, I'm serious. Even through the two inches of polyester fill in that gaudy getup you're wearing, I can tell your body is still as good as ever."

So, he still thought of her purely in terms of her skiing potential: how strong the muscles, how limber the joints, how trim the vehicle in which she would ride to the winner's platform. Apparently he had long ago forgotten how important it had been to her that her body please him after they left the ski slopes. When they were back at their hotel, or in their rooms at whatever lodge they were currently inhabiting, she'd never been too tired for more lessons, she'd never ceased her efforts to please him. She blushed slightly, remembering how willing she had been as he initiated her into that other world of competition, where each partner tried to outdo the other in offering comfort and pleasure to the other. But all he remembered was her body as an instrument for winning medals.

He continued his scan, his eyes moving over every inch of her bright new yellow ski suit.

"And I can tell by those ski clothes that you're doing very well. Apparently life is going well for you."

"Money is no problem, if that's what you mean," she said, boldly lying and hoping that this was another of those times when she could fool him.

"I wish you had asked me for more when you left. You had money coming to you; we'd worked hard for it."

"I didn't want money . . . I . . ."

"I know, you were in a big hurry to re-marry and all you wanted was the quickest, smoothest divorce you could get. I guess my money didn't mean much to you. All you took was my pride. Well, I hope things worked out just the way you wanted them to."

She was surprised to hear that trace of bitterness still left in his reactions to their parting. She was shaken to realize that she might have hurt him, and that he hadn't forgotten.

"And what about you?" she asked, trying to keep the tremor from her voice that she knew would give away her distress. "You've kept up on your skiing, I can see that. I didn't observe many changes in you, either."

She looked down at the clumsy skiers on the slope below her and remembered the self-assured figure she'd just followed down the hill. He hadn't put on any weight, and he still held his long torso with the same elegant bearing of a young professional athlete, although by now he was over thirty-five years of age, for he was a decade older than she was.

It was his face that interested her. She knew that was where she'd be able to read the real history of the days since she'd last seen him. She turned to look at him, but he was wearing dark glasses with a reflective coating that made it seem as if she were looking into a fun-house mirror. She could see her own face, distorted into a phony exaggerated smile, staring back at her.

She reached up and placed her hands on each side of his face at his temples and pulled the glasses from his face, the familiarity of the gesture seeming entirely natural to her. It was as if she were raising the curtain on a drama of unexpected poignancy, for Grant's face had, indeed, changed. She could see that as soon as the glasses were away from his face and she could stare at him unimpeded.

Mentally she traced the features of his face, just as she had done so often with her fingers during those romantic times when her favorite pastime had been the exploration of Grant Mitchell. But now, though she found the strong bone structure that gave his face such sharp planes of strength unchanged, the skin surfaces seemed to have been buffeted and pummeled by circumstances and experience until they were toughened, more resistant, and somewhat damaged. There were lines at the corners of his eyes, and as he returned her studious look, more lines appeared like a shadow just beneath his dark eyes. His jet-black hair had been softened, too, by time, for there was mixed into it now the bright shine of a coarse silver hair here and there.

He was, if it were possible, more handsome than he had ever been as a young man, because his deep eyes now seemed to be hinting that they had witnessed terrible torments, unspeakable delights, a wealth of events worth retelling if only the observer cared to dip further into his psyche. Cared to share with him . . .

"Why are you staring at me like that?" he asked her, and then as if to answer his own question he put his arm around the back of her chair and leaned closer to her.

Felicia's eyes flared with shock as she realized that he thought she was waiting to be kissed. He had misinterpreted her absorbed curiosity as desire, and he seemed willing to satisfy her, even in this awkwardly

31

public place. He took his other hand from the steel pole that rose between their chairs like the support of a carousel horse and took hold of her chin to pull her face toward his.

He was still wearing his black ski gloves, and his touch was impersonal through the stiff leather, but her face pressed willingly forward to meet his, and when their lips touched, Felicia felt as if the ski lift had suddenly stopped still in midair. She heard no more sounds around her, was conscious of no one watching them, did not know or care whether their chair was approaching the crest of the hill. She was only aware of the memories aroused by the familiar touch of Grant's lips.

Perhaps she had been curious, perhaps she had been subconsciously willing his mouth to hers, just to see if that same heady passion could be evoked again in her cold body. In the years since she'd seen Grant, she'd come to believe that her senses were too dead to be provoked. No man seemed capable of duplicating the effect Grant had once had upon her. And now she was thrilled to discover that the problem was not within herself. She was still alive inside, despite what she'd feared. Grant's lips were the keys that were needed to open those majestic doorways of desire, just as they had been before.

Felicia heard a gruff warning, and then felt a slap of cold air on her lips as Grant jerked away from her.

"Tips up. Get those tips up, folks," the attendant at the lift terminal was calling, and she turned with a flustered look to see that their chair was rapidly moving toward the dismounting area. But she did not have her ski poles correctly positioned and her arm was caught around the center support pole where it had been reaching toward Grant.

The attendant did not seem surprised. This was not the first time he'd encountered a romantic couple who'd become distracted during the ride up the mountain. If Grant and Felicia couldn't disengage themselves in time to get out of the chairs safely, he would merely push a button and stop the chair lift all the way down the mountain until they were out of the way. But Felicia knew he'd also offer an embarrassing admonition to pay more attention next time, so she hurried to lift her ski tips up where they wouldn't catch on the platform of hard-packed snow and shift her weight forward to make her exit from the chair just as if she'd had her mind where it should be.

"Are you all right? Do you have your poles?" Grant asked in a concerned rush of words as he eased up out of his chair and began to step to the side.

"Yes, yes. I'm fine," she replied, hurrying to get out of the chair so she wouldn't hold up all the skiers coming up the hill behind her. But she didn't notice that the basket at the bottom of one of her ski poles had caught on the edge of the chair, and as she lunged forward it pulled her off-balance before it came loose.

She struggled to get control of the skis under her feet, and she began to head down the incline off of the chair with Grant reaching out to balance her. But it was too late. She fell over like a rank beginner, clutching at Grant in a last-ditch attempt to save herself so that he fell on top of her and two of them slid in a tumble of skis and poles down the short slope.

When they reached the bottom, they automatically crawled off of the path so that the next chairload of skiers could skim past them, and then leaned back half buried in the snow and smirked at each other, sharing their ignominious moment.

Grant began to laugh, the mirth lighting up his face so that all the care that she'd been reading into it instantly disappeared and she wondered if she'd only imagined it.

Each couple coming off the chair behind them skied past, watching them with amusement, for she and Grant were making no attempt to right themselves. They simply sat in the snow, skis and poles a fallen forest of confusion around them, laughing together at former ski catastrophes.

"You know, I remember something like this happening to us once before, at Park City, wasn't it?" he said.

"And how about that time at Mammoth? You were whispering dirty words in my ear, and we forgot to get off the chair, and after they shut it down, they couldn't get it started again. No one would speak to us for a week!" Felicia was laughing harder than she'd laughed in months, remembering their reputation as the reckless lovers of the ski slopes.

Grant had pulled her into the snowbank, and now his arm was caught beneath her back. She began to feel it move slightly beneath her, just as it had in the old days when she'd fallen asleep sprawled across it so that it became numb during the night. His face came close to hers as he pulled his arm free with another burst of laughter that ruffled at her hair.

"I'm just glad your husband didn't catch us at this one," Grant said, and the laughter suddenly stopped.

"What?" Felicia asked stupidly.

"What would he have thought if he'd seen you kissing your former husband on the chair lift? I presume he's here with you."

"No, the whole family couldn't come together. He couldn't make it. He's not here. He didn't come along this time."

Felicia fumbled through the snow, found Grant's dark glasses and handed them to him, found the straps to her poles, and stood up to begin brushing snow off of her clothing.

"Well, then since I've caught you momentarily unescorted, suppose we go into the Round House for some lunch."

"But that's sinful. Two runs before lunch? I've never had such a lazy day of skiing."

"Did you get a late start?"

"Yes, I had to drop someone off at the ski school over on Dollar Mountain and wait for the lessons to start. So by the time I got over here, it was later than I usually like to begin."

"Well, you're not in training any more, so don't worry about it. Let me buy you some of that chili you used to like so much."

Without waiting for her agreement,

36

Grant unfolded his tall frame up out of the snow and nonchalantly skied away as if nothing unusual had happened during his ride up the first half of the mountain.

They ate their grilled-cheese sandwiches and bowls of chili on the outside porch at the Round House, pausing occasionally as everyone else did to take in the spectacular view of descending mountaintops around them. It was a perfect skiing day, with the temperature about twenty-five degrees so that the snow stayed powdery, and yet there was no wind, and a bright sun made it seem warm even sitting outside with their jackets off.

Felicia ate fast, anxious to get the meal over with and get back to skiing behind Grant down Exhibition again. She hoped to get in a few good runs after lunch before she'd have to hurry back to the lodge. But Grant was more relaxed and took the time to answer her questions about what he'd been doing in great detail.

"I'm not doing any more coaching. Haven't done that in years. I've gotten into the development of ski lodges, and I've become enough of an expert that I'm called in to advise on all kinds of projects. I bought a small lodge in the Black Forest. Then, there's a new place going in near Val

Gardena in Italy that I'll probably be consulting on. And remember our trip to Saint Moritz? Well, I have invested in a project just south of where we stayed."

"So you're in Europe most of the time?"

"Yes, but right now I'm touring this country, visiting as many resorts as I can to gather ideas. I saw Billy Kidd at Steamboat Springs. Oh, and Stein Eriksen is at that new development in Utah. I visited there recently."

Felicia hooked behind her ears the long blond strands of hair that kept swinging forward into her face and leaned forward on the table to study Grant as he talked. Obviously he was still leading the carefree type of life that he enjoyed. He was traveling all over the world, visiting all the glamour spots where the elite of the ski world gathered. He was probably still staying up too late, forgetting meals now and then, trying to do too much, crowding too much into his days. That accounted for the intriguing new signs of dissipation she'd noticed in his face. But he was living exactly as he wanted to live, and that was what was important. He was five years older than when she'd last seen him, but he was still just the same.

Finally having finished his lunch, and

tired of doing all the talking, Grant leaned back in his chair and stretched his long legs out in front of him so that they stuck out on the other side of the table.

"I'm glad to have seen you, Felicia. You know, I've tried to find out how you're doing, but that brother of yours will never tell me a damn thing. He never told me your new name, never told me where you were living."

She had wondered if he ever thought about her. But Phil had never mentioned Grant's inquiries. To be fair about it, she had to remind herself that she'd made Phil swear never to mention Grant to her again. She turned away from his darkly analyzing look. She didn't answer him because she wanted to avoid any discussion of her own life, and she dumped dishes back on the trays, hoping he wouldn't notice her reticence.

"Are you going to be here all week?" he asked crisply, standing up from the table so unexpectedly that Felicia began hastily collecting her parka from the chair beside her.

"Why yes. Are you?"

"Probably. Unless I get called back to Europe. Well, I'll no doubt run into you again, then. I promised to help a friend try out some new longer skis this afternoon. See you later."

She watched him leave the deck of the Round House, his long, purposeful strides so typical of him, the slim intensity of his body perfectly portraying his hunger to get on with what he was doing, to get himself quickly back in the middle of all the action.

She remained sitting for a moment, her blue eyes misted with a fond understanding of him that she blinked rapidly away. After all, she reminded herself with rising anger, he'd just given her the brush-off. One run down Exhibition and a bowl of chili! That was all she got for the years of waiting and wondering what it would be like if she ever saw him again. Now she could spend the years ahead remembering this day at Sun Valley: laughing about their fall from the chair lift, remembering what it was like to kiss him again, being glad that she'd decided to leave him five years ago.

As she rebuckled the top closure of her new ski boots and left the Round House to find her skis, she decided that she would go directly to Exhibition and ski it alone to prove to herself that she didn't need to have Grant to follow. She could have just as much fun skiing alone, she tried to convince herself. If Grant could treat their reunion so lightly, dashing off to meet some snow bunny he'd made a date with for the

40

afternoon, then she could just as easily put it from her mind.

Unfortunately Felicia was too distracted to ski well on her next run. She'd just had a disturbing collision with her past, and it had left her with fresh scars which throbbed painfully in her mind. And the tender old bruises which had never healed cried out for her attention as well. So she skied to the bottom of River Run, crossed the bridge over Wood River, and headed for the parking lot.

When she got on the bus, she was happy to see the older man she'd shared one lift ride with. Based on that brief encounter, they now greeted each other like old friends.

"You're quitting a little early, aren't you?" he asked.

"Well, my little girl is having her first ski lesson over on Half Dollar, and I must admit I can't wait to get over there and see how she's doing," Felicia said.

"They have the best ski school in the world here. I'm sure she's doing just fine. Maybe in a few years she'll be skiing as well as that man in black that we watched on Exhibition. Wasn't he something?" The man whistled a stream of sound between his teeth in astonished memory of Grant's

41

beautifully executed run.

"I could have watched him ski all day," she said quietly, remembering those long legs gripping the skis for control, and the black-clad hips swiveling from side to side in rhythmic, wide undulations against the shimmering snow. "That man is one of the most beautiful skiers I've ever seen," she said, grateful for the opportunity to speak frankly with this stranger.

"Oh, I don't know. I caught sight of a yellow flash down that mountain a few minutes ago that was awfully nice to watch. You ski like a real pro."

"I raced on the World Cup circuit for a couple of years."

"I thought so. You have the look of a well-trained skier. But now you just ski on vacations and the rest of the time devote yourself to being a wife and mother, is that it?" he asked with interest.

"I spend a lot of time with my little girl, yes. But I work in a ski shop and stay in touch with the ski world that way. I usually get on skis every winter, leading tours for the ski shop."

"Well, here's the lodge where I get off. See you on Baldy tomorrow. Just wait till I tell my wife I met a beautiful Nordic goddess who was a ski racer," he chuckled to himself as he left the bus.

As she bounced along on the short road that led out to the beginners' ski area, she tried to resurrect the pride she used to feel about the successful days of her ski competition. She'd had a lot to be happy about in those days: a husband and coach whom she loved, a life of excitement and travel, satisfying work as she constantly refined her skills.

If only she hadn't taken that bad fall on the last race of the season. She'd gone on with the team for the summer training program in Aspen, and even though her leg still bothered her, she'd tried to keep up with the program of long distance and sprint running, agility training, and cycling. By the time they moved on to Portillo, Chile, for August skiing, she was exhausted. Then Grant had ordered her off her skis. During her recuperation she'd had too much time to think and exaggerate her discontentment. With the skiing taken away from her, she'd looked around with restless longings, and it had seemed to her she had little else in her life.

The sharp details so vividly coming back to her caused her to press her hands up to her forehead with a futile attempt to block out the invasion of memories. Heartrending scenes flashed through her mind of that terrible day when everything ended. The visit to the kind American doctor for a physical examination. The phone call she'd overheard in her hotel room. And then the letter she'd written and tucked into Grant's suitcase before he left for Germany for the opening meet of the new season. She said she'd come along later, but she'd never seen him again. Not until today.

She had seen the opportunity for a better life, for the security and permanence she'd always wanted, and she'd taken that chance. And the following years, while less exciting and less filled with wonder, had been fulfilling in their own way. And she rarely allowed herself to revisit and ponder the past. No regrets, she told herself as the bus pulled up at Dollar Mountain.

"Mommy, Mommy. There you are. Why didn't you come sooner? You could have seen me ski. I can really ski, just like you do."

Sally came crunching toward her through the snow, half dragging her tiny skis behind her. The child was crusted with snow, right up to the huge red pom-pom atop her stocking cap.

"You look like a melting snowman, darling. Come and get on the bus. We'll go back to the lodge and have some hot chocolate in our room."

"But, Mommy, when are you going to see me ski?"

"Tomorrow morning, first thing. In fact, maybe I'll ski with you. I want to see what you've learned."

"See, my teacher calls this leg peanut butter, and this leg jelly," Sally was puffing out her words as she loaded her skis into the bus rack and let her mother usher her aboard. As Felicia removed her mittens for her, the child chattered on, to the delight of the other adults on the bus.

"And then he yells at me to put my weight on peanut butter, or put it on jelly. What's that mean, Mommy? What does he mean to put my weight on it?"

Felicia laughed with delight. The clever teaching method had apparently been wasted on her adorable little girl. She pulled the hat off of Sally's head, smoothed the wispy brown hair softly into place, and whispered into her ear, "I'll show you tomorrow, my sweet. We'll peanut butter and jelly together all day tomorrow."

When they were back in their rooms at the lodge, Felicia popped her daughter into a warm bubble bath and began peeling off her own layers of ski clothes. She jumped with a start when the phone by the bed rang.

"Felicia, this is Grant. Sorry I had to run off and leave you so quickly today. How about dinner tonight?"

Felicia was caught by surprise, and she stood with her open mouth motionless near the mouthpiece of the phone, her free hand twisting a strand of her blond hair nervously.

Grant spoke more slowly when he began again.

"I'm sorry, it was thoughtless of me to spring that on you so abruptly. You said your husband wasn't with you, and there are some business matters we need to discuss. So I simply wondered if we could eat together tonight."

"I don't know, Grant."

Some instinct deep in her heart flashed a warning light, telling her that she should avoid seeing him tonight or ever again.

"Are you afraid that your husband will object?" he asked with a rough abrasion to his voice. "I can guarantee we'll be only in the most public places. No harm will come to your reputation, you can assure him of that."

"It's not that. It's just that I have my little girl with me. I would need a sitter and I don't know . . ."

Her words faltered to a stop and then there was a moment of silence as Grant said nothing.

She ventured a few more words into the void to complete her thought. "I think it's too late to find a sitter for the baby."

Grant's voice was cold, all the bursting enthusiasm of a few moments ago seeming to have been removed. He had always hated making plans, thinking ahead, complications. He doubtless considered her child an annoyance, a burdensome detail which had spoiled all the spontaneity of his plans for the evening.

"The manager here is a friend of mine," he said. "I'll tell him to send up a baby-sitter at seven o'clock. Meet me at the front desk." He hung up the phone without any further formalities.

She knew that Grant was probably surprised she'd had a child. He'd always thought of her as a mere child herself, too young to take on the responsibilities of a settled home-life. His aloof attitude was just what she might have expected.

When the knock on the door came promptly at seven, Sally was just finishing off the plate of meat loaf her mother had ordered for her from room service. As Felicia introduced her to the off-duty waitress named Mary who would stay with her, she noticed that Sally's head was bobbing over the piece of cake she was trying to eat for dessert.

"She's so tired she can't even finish that," Felicia told the sitter, who was settling into a chair with some books. "I'll get her into bed before I leave," she added, pulling down the blankets and turning out the bedside light.

"Mommy, where are you going?"

"Out to dinner, dear. I won't be gone long."

"Are you going by yourself?"

"No, dear, with a friend."

"A girl friend?" Sally asked as she climbed up onto the bed.

"No, a man I used to know."

"Is he a nice man, Mommy?"

"Yes."

"Can I meet him sometime?" she yawned.

"We'll see."

"Why do you always say 'we'll see' when you mean 'no,' Mommy?"

"That's just what mothers say, I guess."

"Have fun with the nice man, Mommy." Sally's eyes were closed already, and she wiggled her head about on the pillow, snuggling in.

Sally, baby, if only I could tell you! If only I could come right out and tell you the truth and say, 'Sleep well, my darling. Mother's just going out to have dinner with your father.' But I can't tell you that he's your father. And I certainly can't tell him. Not ever.

CHAPTER THREE

Felicia was wearing the white cowl-necked cashmere sweater that had, in a way, been a Christmas present from her mother. Actually her mother had sent her a silver chafing dish from one of the most expensive gift shops in Vail, apparently picturing Felicia hostessing elegant little buffet dinners the way she did herself during the winter social season. Felicia had mailed the gift back to the store, asked for a refund, and with the money had bought her daughter two dresses, paid the next month's tuition at the daycare center, and found the sweater for herself at an after-Christmas sale.

Now she slipped over the sweater a shiny purple après-ski jacket that Dan Fowler, the manager of Fun Sports, had asked her to try out for him, and she frowned slightly at the effect. The jacket had an unflattering dyed fur trimming at the collar and the color was not right with the beige velvet jeans from her own wardrobe, but she wore it anyway because it looked luxurious, and she wanted Grant Mitchell to go on believing that she was well taken care of.

Grant was standing in the main lobby, tapping one foot impatiently. "There you are. What held you up? Was there some problem?"

"Oh, yes. You know how children are. There's always some terrible last-minute crisis to deal with, or some complication to drive you crazy." Actually, she was late because she'd been fussing with her hair for ten minutes.

"If there's any real problem, go ahead and take care of it. We can eat somewhere else."

"What do you mean?"

"I made reservations for the Trail Creek Cabin, but we have to catch the sleigh at seven fifteen."

"Oh, I remember Trail Creek," Felicia said, the fondness of her remembrance showing in her voice before she could stop it. "No, the problems are all resolved and I think the baby's settled down now. But we'd better run for that sleigh."

She bolted for the door like a prisoner finally set free. She hadn't been out to dinner to an exciting place, all dressed up, for a long time, and she felt girlish again in these surroundings where once she had reveled in her youth and freedom. She almost pranced as she headed down the front steps and off toward the picturesque square in front of the opera house where the horse-drawn sled was waiting.

"Slow down, the driver can see we're coming. He'll wait," Grant admonished as if he were escorting an impetuous child. "Felicia, be careful."

Just as if he had predicted it, her foot slipped on a patch of ice and her next step carried her a foot farther than it should have. She waved her arms to catch herself, and Grant quickly stepped behind her to put his hands under her arms and steady her.

"I'm all right. Really, you can let go." But while her words instructed him to let her loose, her body was giving him other messages. She let herself fall back against him, loving the feeling of leaning on someone so tall and protective. She had been in sole charge of her own life for so long that she welcomed the feeling of being held in the custody of someone stronger, someone who was watching out for her so that she could forget her responsibilities for awhile and be reckless and adventurous.

"Come on, last one in has to pay for dinner," she teased, pulling from his firm hold to begin running again toward the wagon. She grabbed for the driver's helping hand and stepped aboard.

When she was on top of the wagon, she turned to look for Grant, and she was surprised to see that he was still standing in the same spot where he had held her so briefly. His eyes caught the light of a nearby streetlamp, and she thought she was seeing old fires ablaze again for a moment. He looked immovable, the wind carrying heavy strands of dark hair in a wavering pattern across his forehead, his lips slightly parted as if he were about to call out.

She imagined a quick fantasy scene in which Grant would command her to get down off the sleigh and come back to him, forget about dinner, and do as she was told. The picture in her mind brought a smile to her face as she saw herself thrown over his strong shoulder and carried away by him, but just then a raucous voice burst into her improbable dream.

"Hey, there's my little ski buddy who kept getting lost on the mountain today. Come on, Felicia, honey. Sit right here on the other side of old Joe."

Joe Posten had one arm around a pert little redhead and the other extended toward Felicia. Since there were few spaces left on the benches that lined the length of

53

the wagon, she took a seat beside him, indicating to Grant with a nodding gesture that there was plenty of room beside her for him. Grant moved up onto the wagon with one giant stride of his long legs, and sat down and put his arm around Felicia so confidently and casually that Joe Posten dropped his arm and turned his attention back to the girl on his other side.

Several of the passengers were already tuning up their voices, trying out the first lines of songs to the others to get some singing going. The driver passed around bags of popcorn and then climbed up on the front seat and clicked his horses to attention. With a jangle of the sleigh bells that decorated their harness, the horses stepped forward into the dark night to begin the trip to the famous old lodge a few miles out in the country. The mood was highly charged with gaiety, and Felicia felt herself drawn into the romantic perfection of the scene.

"How about a little drink, Felicia?" Joe asked her. "You do it like this." He took off the leather boda bag he was wearing on a strap over his shoulder and leaned his head back to squirt red wine directly into his mouth from a few inches away.

"I'll try it!" Felicia said, feeling ready to

try any new experience this evening. Grant smiled at her as she took a drink without spilling a drop and passed the bag on to him.

"That's no fair," he chided her. "You held it too close. It's more of a challenge this way."

He held it at arm's length, and stretched his long tan neck forward to meet the stream of wine he was aiming expertly down his throat. After a lusty swig or two he gave the bag back to Joe. Grant thanked him in a friendly manner, but Felicia noticed that he didn't go out of his way to converse with him any more after that, and as soon as the sleigh had reached its destination, he took her by the hand to lead her in the opposite direction from Joe and his redhead.

As soon as they were inside the rustic old brown building that housed the Trail Creek restaurant, Grant led her to a fireside table for two. He pulled off his lambskin coat revealing its lining of soft curly lamb's wool as he placed it on his chair. Then he said to her with a scowl, "Let me help you take off that jacket."

He came to stand behind her chair and held the sleeves as she slipped out her arms. Then, holding the mass of purple between thumb and forefinger as if it were contaminated somehow, he dropped it on a nearby chair.

"That thing looks terrible on you," he said.

"I didn't pick it out, so you aren't offending me, if that's what you're trying to do. It was a gift."

"Well, your husband has terrible taste," he said, curling his upper lip in disgust.

"It wasn't from my husband."

"Oh, you take expensive gifts from others?"

She couldn't maintain the ruse any longer. She knew that sooner or later she was bound to slip, so she might as well eliminate the mystery man from the story right now.

"My husband and I no longer live together, Grant," she said.

"What? I can't believe that. The love match of the century, and it didn't last?" He gave her a look that showed how truly shocked he was, then raked his hands through his dark straight hair. "Good God, Felicia. That makes you a two-time loser. You couldn't make it with me, and now you've left him? What is it with you?"

"They do say that sometimes there's more than one person to blame when a marriage breaks up. And, well, I guess I'm just not the marriageable type. I should have stayed single," she said, keeping her eyes on her hands which were clasped in her lap. She hoped her words carried an air of conviction.

"Except for your baby, of course."

"Oh, yes. I couldn't think of life without her. But I enjoy my independence. Making my own decisions, that sort of thing." She gave a tight, strained little laugh that lacked sincerity.

"A tough-minded Swede, that's what you are."

"Thank you for not calling me a blockheaded Swede, like you used to."

"I hope this guy settled plenty of money on you, leaving you with a child to support and all. If it was his fault, if he walked out and left you, I hope you socked it to him for plenty."

"Oh, I did, believe me. I'm well taken care of."

Felicia felt her eyebrows rise up to hide amongst the long bangs that covered her forehead as she looked into Grant's eyes, praying that her performance was convincing. She wished she could hide from him completely, for only then was she sure she could keep the truth from him. This facing him head on for the first time in five years was making her extremely uneasy.

Grant was looking at her with a slightly dubious expression, and he had just started to open his mouth to say something when the waitress came up to take their order.

"I think I'll have the steak," she told Grant.

He turned to the waitress. "She'll have the top sirloin, medium rare. I'll have the fresh trout. And two salads with Roquefort dressing. Oh, and a bottle of California Zinfandel. Bring that right now, please."

"You haven't forgotten a thing. My favorite salad dressing, my favorite wine, the steak just right. How do you remember all that with the hectic life you lead?" She was sincere in her flattery, for he had dazzled her by almost duplicating the meal they had shared here over seven years ago, right after they first met.

"I haven't forgotten one thing about my life with you, Felicia. I savor it all. You must remember, I was the one who was happy. I was the one living in the fool's paradise, too stupid to know what was about to hit me." He leaned on the table, thrusting himself toward her so that she could not miss the anger that smoldered in his brown eyes. "I thought I was making you happy. At least you woke up every morning with a smile on your face. But maybe that was because you'd been dreaming about him."

"You must have known that the life we were leading couldn't go on forever. That wasn't marriage; it was two people roaming the world, just living side by side."

"I liked it."

"I know you did. To do what you like to do best, you have to live that way. But I wanted more."

"Then why didn't you tell me? I mean before it was too late, before he came along."

"I don't know. Oh, Grant, do we have to talk about this? It's long over and should be forgotten." She was startled herself to hear the sob in her voice, and she could see in Grant's catch of breath a reaction of surprise at her vehemence. She turned her face away from him to study the fire that was burning in the huge stone fireplace beside their table.

Grant's voice was as soothing as a caress when he spoke again, as if deep emotion had rubbed off all the hard edges on his words.

"Just tell me one thing. Was it because I pushed you too hard? That day we were in the waxing room, fixing your skis up before that race when you hurt yourself, I told you not to ski if you didn't want to, remember?"

"Skiing has nothing to do with this. Forget the races and eating at the training table and the muscle-toning exercises, will you? Our problem concerned two people who just weren't in love any more."

"One who wasn't."

"Oh, really?" she challenged, a bitter stab of remembrance making her words harsh. "I wish you'd stop putting all the blame on me. I have reason to believe a lot of love died that summer. But I refuse to talk about it anymore. I'm going to the ladies' room, and I'm only coming back if you promise not to discuss this anymore."

"I said I wanted to talk business. As soon as you've dried your eyes, we'll get down to that."

"There's nothing wrong with my eyes," she protested as he stood up and with a grand bow of gallantry waited for her to leave the table.

When she got to the rest room, she splashed water all over her face, cupping the water around her eyes with her hands to soothe them, and thereby removing every bit of the mascara with which she'd darkened her light lashes. She dried her face thoroughly, and was reassured to see in the mirror that she could appear so composed. Sometimes her stoic Nordic background was a blessing, for the serene openness of her round face in its frame of sunny blond hair belied any suggestion of unhappiness. She managed to radiate vitality, good health, and contentment, no matter what her real condition. She smoothed her hair so that it again looked like a peaceful, sun-splashed waterfall cascading straight toward her shoulders, and she rearranged her bangs over her forehead with her fingers.

"You look better," Grant said as she returned to the table.

He was watching her closely, as if he wanted to measure the temperature of her mood. She vowed that she would not show him any more of the grief in her remembrances; she would hold back the tears while she was with him, even if that meant letting go with a deluge when she was back in her room away from him. Sally had seen her cry before, it would not upset her unduly.

A western-style combo had appeared at the opposite end of the dance floor, facing the fireplace. Of course the first number on the program was "It Happened in Sun Valley," and no one wanted to miss that one so the floor was becoming crowded.

"Shall we dance?" Grant asked her softly. "It's safer than talking, I think. We were always most happy when we were doing something active together." He gave her a look that seemed heavy with innuendo, but she wondered if she just imagined what he had meant.

At first Felicia positioned herself rather demurely in his arms, then she realized how conspicuous they must appear, like grade schoolers at their first dancing class. Gradually she let herself settle into a more intimate position against him, her eyelashes brushing together close to his chin.

"Is that one of your famous butterfly kisses I feel?" Grant mumbled in a husky whisper. One of their private jokes had been his growling reaction of pleasure whenever he felt her long lashes sweeping against his skin.

She didn't answer him but cautiously moved her face, feeling in her neck the strain of trying to hold her head away from him. The close body contact was having a more stimulating effect on her than she would have imagined, and she concentrated intently on the melody of the song, trying to anticipate how soon it would be over and she could suggest they return to the table.

Typical of large men with the well-tuned bodies of athletes, Grant was a graceful and responsive dancer and his sense of rhythm was infallible. He led her so confidently that she could forget her steps and enjoy the music. Now as the musicians increased their tempo for a big finish, Grant pressed her more closely to him so that he could twirl them in time to the music. Her long legs moved identically to his, their length pressed against him. Her breasts were crushed against his broad chest so tightly that she couldn't be sure if it was his heartbeat or her own that she felt. And her hips, fitted against his as if formed from the opposite pieces of a mold, responded with a pleasurable throb to his closeness, reminding her of what further moments of delight could come from that yearning for fusion.

She could feel the hot moistness under her hair at the back of her neck, and feel her breath accelerating fast, racing the beat of the music. She began to fear that if the dance went on much longer, she would make a fool of herself. She was putting her hand too close to the flame as she played with this fire. She could ruin her life, and her daughter's, if she were to lose control, blurt out long tangled stories full of the truth, for once, as she wanted to do. She pushed herself away from him, her eyes glazed with the madness of suppressed emotion, but the music was almost over so her abrupt move did not appear unusual.

"You seem anxious to get back to the table," Grant said as he released her from his arms. "Have you developed that much interest in wine? Or is it just that you've lost all interest in the other pleasures we used to share?" he added with an ugly sardonic twist to his words.

As she stared up at him in the middle of the dance floor, she wondered what happens to all the emotions that are left over after a great love fades away. Do they simply die with it, or is it possible to revive small embers, puff them into life again for a moment? Here in this romantic atmosphere, her life, by coincidence, at a crossroads point that made her feel especially lonely and vulnerable, she seemed to be doing just that, grasping at small, residual feelings from her past for comfort, and she knew that she must stop.

"Since our wine is at the table," she said, maintaining a surprising amount of coolness in her tone, "shall we give a toast to this unexpected reunion, to this opportunity to put our past to rest once and for all?"

"That's all that's left for us, isn't it? Burying the bones."

He filled their glasses when they returned to the table and then stared into his with a bleak expression that made her feel as if she'd been suddenly submerged in an ice-water pond.

Soon they were occupied with their dinner and the well-rehearsed good humor of the western-style MC and his comedy routine. She refused all Grant's further suggestions that they join the dancing, even when it was a most proper round dance, begging off with the excuse that this was the first day of her vacation and she was tired.

Actually she used the time while he was watching the other dancers to consider the week ahead. If Grant didn't suddenly jet off to someplace across the continent, and remained in Sun Valley, she would have to discourage any further social contacts between them. But he was still likely to encounter her with Sally.

She hastily added up months and years and calculated dates in her mind. When she left Grant, she had been only two months pregnant. Sally was now nearly four and a half, so when asked her age, she held up four fingers very proudly. Thank

God, thought Felicia, her daughter was not one of those children who sing out that the half-way mark in her age would soon be reached.

Grant turned to see her eyes darting around the room in time to her rapid thought processes, her mind obviously not upon the organized frivolity of the western party.

"Would you like to leave? You don't seem very interested in this."

"Oh, yes. As a matter of fact, the noise is beginning to get to me. I guess I'm tired."

"I imagine with a baby to take care of, you have to get up quite early."

"Oh, I can't really call Sally a baby any more," she said with forced lightness. "Not now that she's turned four." Felicia hated the lying most of all, and this time she turned her face away to avoid the scrutiny of his eyes. "But she still gets up early."

"Your child is four years old?" Grant stopped buttoning his jacket and stood regarding her with a hostile expression. "Boy, you and that sex fiend you married didn't wait long, did you?"

"We wanted a family. We didn't see any point in putting it off."

"You barely waited for the ink to dry on those divorce papers before you were in

66

bed with another man."

"I don't think I have to make explanations to you."

"If not to me, Felicia, then who else would give a damn? I was the injured party."

"Injured party? I'm sure that long before I ever remarried you were off in Europe somewhere, bundled up with the entire women's French ski team."

"Whatever gave you that idea?"

"Face it, Grant. Our marriage was a disaster. There was no trust, no permanence, no . . . no . . ."

"No love? You can't convince me of that."

She stood up and slipped into the awful purple parka, glad that the activity around them had masked the intensity of their conversation. No one seemed the least aware that two lives were being dissected here in front of the fire.

The driver of the sled seemed surprised that anyone would want to leave the party so early, and planned to wait for more passengers before returning to the village, but Grant slipped him a bill that changed his mind. They were alone in the wagon; but while the driver kept his glance discreetly forward toward his horses, suspecting their intense urge to return to their quarters to be for the more typical reasons he usually encountered, she and Grant sat separated by several inches of icy draft.

They stepped from the sleigh ride into the square of Alpine buildings, frosted like iced gingerbread houses with the white roof-drifts of snow. As they walked, Grant clapped his gloved hands together to warm them.

"I told you we have business to discuss. So, let's get in out of the cold someplace and get it over with." He gave a deep sigh which seemed to indicate he was as anxious as she was to finish this painful meeting. He had obviously pronounced their relationship to be as hopeless as Felicia had and would be glad when he could find an excuse to leave Sun Valley and be back in the exciting world of skiers and business investments and away from the domestic quarrels she reminded him of.

"Look, I didn't get my coffee out there at Trail Creek and I could use something to warm me up. Wouldn't you like something?"

They had paused on the sidewalk right in front of the Ram, and from inside the café she could hear the entrancing tinkle of the zither player entertaining.

"All right. Just for a while. I do have a

68

baby-sitter to account to."

As soon as they were seated in one of the deep wooden-sided booths that afforded them the privacy their discussion might require, Grant ordered two Irish coffees. They pulled off their heavy outer garments and sat listening to the haunting strains of a Tyrolean melody being picked out on the zither.

"Do you remember our house?"

Felicia almost slipped off the slick wooden bench of the booth she was so startled by Grant's abrupt question.

"What do you mean, our house? We lived in one crazy hotel room after another. I don't think we ever slept under the roof of a real home."

"Don't you remember the house we planned? You know, when we bought that hunting lodge up in the Sierras. We spent many a night in front of the fire sketching dream houses with a chunk of charcoal."

"Oh, that's right. The lodge was right at the foot of a beautiful mountain, and you wanted to turn it into a base lodge for skiers."

"And we were going to build a house nearby. All glass, lots of windows looking out to the slopes, remember? That was going to be for us."

"I'd almost forgotten."

"Well, you own it, you know."

"I own it?"

"Yes. That stupid brother of yours! When he was handling your divorce, he didn't ask me for any support payments. My lawyer practically had to force him to ask for half of our community property. All he took was that piece of mountain property for you."

The waitress brought their glasses of coffee with whipped cream on top, and Grant picked his up and took a large swallow. Then he wiped the whipped cream from his lips with an impatient blot from the back of his hand and continued. "I guess you knew you were latching onto a new husband with so much money that you didn't care what you took with you from our marriage."

In truth Felicia had told Phil not to ask for any monthly support from Grant because she didn't want to be tied to him in any continuing way so that he might learn her whereabouts and come after her. Despite her brother's advice, she'd insisted she wanted nothing from her divorce. She was young and strong and felt sure that she could support herself. Of course, she'd been naïve then; she hadn't realized how difficult it would be to put her child into the hands of strangers for care when it was only six weeks old so that she could take a job to support the two of them.

"Quite honestly, Grant, I'd forgotten all about that piece of property. I guess my brother has the deed somewhere with my legal papers."

"Well, I haven't forgotten it. I've kept track of it. There was a problem with putting in ski lifts, if you remember. I have a file of correspondence this thick with the Forest Service about it. Then, just a month or two ago, I received word that it has been okayed for development."

"You mean, it can be turned into a ski resort now?"

"Yes, you own a valuable piece of land, Felicia, not that you need it."

"You mean, I could sell it now, and for a good price?"

The idea lit her eyes up with a sparkle of bright excitement. Maybe this was the answer she was looking for. She had come to Sun Valley to think about her future, and now perhaps she could go home and quit her job, say good-bye to Dan Fowler and Fun Sports, and live off of her real estate profits for awhile, taking time to be with her daughter.

Grant had put down his hot glass and was sitting quite still, studying her reaction. He interrupted her happy jumble of thoughts to caution her, "Not so fast, now. To sell it right away would be a big mistake. We're probably the only two people in the world who know the real potential of that property. We know how skiable that mountain is, what a beautiful resort Deer Meadow could be."

"Deer Meadow." As she repeated the name, she was flooded with memories of that weekend in the Sierras, the dreams they'd spun. "We flew over it by helicopter, didn't we? Remember that real estate man? He kept telling us about the great hunting we could do near there. And all we could do was stare at that mountain and think about the day when we could strap on skis and go down that two-thousand-foot vertical drop. Oh, it was beautiful! Covered with powder in early December."

"That was my Christmas present to you that year: eight hundred acres wrapped up in a big white bow."

"I can't sell it, you're right."

"For sentimental reasons?"

"For business reasons. That area should be developed. I have to wait for someone to come along who can see that." Felicia's heart was beating faster as she realized the possibilities.

"The way you cherish the past warms my heart," he said with obvious sarcasm.

"I have a child to think about. I have to be practical and businesslike. There's no time for pressing old corsages or gluing dance programs in scrapbooks."

"I thought husband number two left you with plenty of cash," he said through narrowed lips.

"I look out for myself, as well. Now that Sally's almost school age, I have a job. I like to contribute to our welfare."

"You work?" Grant hurled that accusation at her as if he'd just discovered she was a convicted felon.

"Yes, I work. My name is still well known in skiing circles, so I'm a valuable asset at a ski shop."

"You sell people boots? You find them long johns in the right size? You tell them how great they look in purple parkas?"

Grant made it sound as if she sold dope, found dates for lonely businessmen, and flattered sick old rich men. Felicia felt tears well up in her eyes, and she bent forward out of his direct line of sight and sipped her coffee. The nip of the whiskey brought her back to life, while the heat of the coffee spread the consolation through her body instantly.

"That is the way I live and I like it," she said defiantly.

"And does your child like it? Separated from you all day long? A baby should be with its mother."

She was in real danger of losing her temper with him, for he had gouged one of her more tender nerves. She grabbed her parka from beside her, and twisting it in her hands, she said, forcing control into her tone, "You are no longer my coach, Grant. Nor are you my husband. You have no right to make judgments about how I live."

She couldn't stay near him a moment longer. She slid out of the booth and left the Ram. He had no business criticizing and condemning the life she had so painstakingly built for herself and her daughter. She had managed to feel like a success until now. But he was making her small accomplishments seem a sham. He was making her feel that she had failed her daughter. His daughter.

To her surprise he followed her from the restaurant and was there to hold her elbow as she executed the icy steps.

"At least let me escort you back to your

room safely. After our spectacular fall from the chair lift today, and that slip you almost took on the ice earlier, I think you may just be accident prone. I'd better go along to protect you."

Again Felicia appreciated having his masterful presence beside her, watching over her, even after the unpleasantness of the just-completed encounter.

"You've put up with a lot from me tonight," Grant mumbled as they walked down the crunchy sidewalks. "I'm sorry if I sounded critical, Felicia. But I'm asking so many questions about your private life because I can't decide what to believe."

He stopped to place his hands on her shoulders and look at her. "I've always had this same problem with you. When I look down into those beautiful big blue eyes, I believe every word you say. I believed that you loved me when we were married. It has been hard to convince myself that was all lies."

Lights from the windows cast a checkerboard pattern of yellow glow on the snowfield near the side of the old hotel. Felicia could see the irises of Grant's eyes flare up, catlike, in the dark. He leaned back against a low wall, knocking off a small portion of the snowy topping that had formed there during the last storm. He pulled out a package of cigarettes and quickly lit one, throwing the extinguished match into the snow as if it were somehow the reason for all his troubles.

Felicia felt a twinge of guilt, knowing that she had caused this fun-loving, happy-go-lucky man some of the only anxious and unhappy moments of his life. She had abandoned him, walked out on him, told him she was choosing another man's love over what he offered. Now that she was older, she knew that no amount of ego could have weathered that rejection unaffected. He had doubtless been hurt, and he probably still hated her for being the instrument of that rejection, for making him doubt himself for the first time.

"I know you won't understand this, Felicia, but there's one more thing I must do. So have patience, with me." He threw the cigarette to the ground.

"Grit your teeth and endure it, just as you did when you were the patient, unhappy little wife, doing her duty in spite of her misery."

Felicia had known he was going to kiss her from the moment he'd stopped walking. The lighting of the cigarette had been mere preamble. But what surprised her was the cruelty of the act. He wrapped his arms around her with an imprisoning hold, as if he were fearful she'd make a break from him, and his mouth was pressed against hers so brutally that she could feel the pressure of his teeth against hers, battering her lips. She felt a moan begin to form in the lowest depths of her throat. He was hurting her, and she needed to protest. But she choked off the sound almost as soon as it had begun, for he seemed to react to it with more ferocity in his assault, his fingers digging into her arms, making rows of small bruises where her skin surrendered to his pressure.

At last, when she had tightened her mouth beneath his to show her refusal to respond to him, he pulled his face back from hers and stared down into her eyes with the frighteningly passionate look of one to whom possession has been denied.

"You can't even fake it anymore, can you?" he charged with a malevolent glower. "I realize that meant nothing to you, that you hated every minute of it, but I had to find out exactly how you feel, and now you've told me, more convincingly than with words."

Felicia backed away from him, holding herself under tight rein, letting him believe she was beyond his reach. When she was far enough away to feel safe, she turned and rushed into the lodge.

The kiss had been a sentence completed, a thought finished, a final word. After five years Grant Mitchell had finally had his opportunity to say good-bye.

CHAPTER FOUR

"Oatmeal here tastes better than oatmeal at home. Why is that, Mommy?"

"What, dear?"

"You're not listening to me," Sally complained. "I said I love Sun Valley. Even the oatmeal is good."

"I'm glad, Sally. Now finish up your breakfast," Felicia told her absently.

"Why are you making a face, Mommy?"

"Because this grapefruit juice is sour, and it hurts my lips." She put the glass in her hand abruptly back down on the table, realizing that her daughter's habit of rapid-fire interrogation had caused her to admit to that painful reminder of the evening spent with her ex-husband. She put one finger to her mouth and stroked the tender curves to which she hadn't even applied lipstick this morning.

"I'm ready. Let's go. Time to ski," Sally said, officiously pulling on her gloves and looking every inch the giant slalom competitor after just one day of ski school.

79

"Come and let me help you put your cap on."

Sally came from her chair to stand obediently beside Felicia's. She was wearing a red one-piece skiing jump suit that had been loaned to them by a Los Angeles manufacturer who wanted the ski shop to carry his line. It matched the outfit Felicia had chosen to try out, except that the adult version had blue and black racing stripes padded with foam rubber down the sleeves and pant legs.

Felicia delayed the eager child a moment to stroke the velvety sheen of her hair. Sally's hair was brown, but with that exception looked just like her mother's, even to the bangs that hung too long in front. She always insisted on having her hair cut exactly the same as her mother's. Felicia gathered the hair into a loose knot with her hand and placed a quick kiss on it before covering it with the knitted cap.

Sally pulled the hat over her ears. "Isn't it time to go? We have to get on the bus."

Felicia took one last sip of coffee in an effort to rouse herself. She'd had a fitful sleep, and she felt less enthusiastic than her daughter about getting out onto the slopes.

"I'm coming," she laughed as she followed

80

her skipping daughter out of the lodge.

"Today I'm going to learn a lot with my own private teacher all to myself. Aren't I? Don't you think I will?"

Sally was singing out questions in her sweetly tuned voice as Felicia pulled a blue cap on over her own hair, taking big gulps of the frosty morning air to shock herself into wakefulness.

Where a few moments before the child had been urging her on, now she was dawdling, and Felicia reached behind her to take her hand and keep her moving. When she started forward again, she realized she was walking straight into an obstruction taller than she was. It was Grant. He'd planted himself perversely on the path in front of her and she bumped into him as inevitably as the *Titanic* into that lethal iceberg.

"Good morning, ladies," Grant said cheerfully.

Since their parting last night he seemed to have put their relationship on a new footing, forcing the upsetting aftershocks into the background as he greeted her impersonally, like a friendly acquaintance. With his skis over his shoulder and the outline of a snow-covered pine tree behind him, he looked as handsome as a ski poster. Even Sally stopped her darting

81

about to stare up at him attentively. Felicia held her daughter's hand tightly, wishing she could whisk her away from this meeting.

"We're just on our way to the slopes, so if you'll let us by . . ."

"Off to Dollar Mountain, are you?"

"My mother is going to give me a skiing lesson. She's a downhill racer, and she's a champion. She has ribbons and medals and things at home. Do you want to see them sometime?"

Grant bent at the waist to reach Sally's eye level. "I know all about your mother's trophies. I was there when she won them."

"Is this your old friend, Mommy? Is this the one you ate dinner with last night?"

"I'm her old friend and . . ."

Felicia quickly interrupted him. "Mr. Mitchell was also the coach of the team I skied on." She wondered if he had been about to introduce himself to Sally as her mother's ex-husband, then decided that surely he wouldn't be so cruel as to confuse a child with that kind of information.

"You were a ski coach? Do you still give lessons?" Sally asked, her round dark eyes showing how impressed she was.

"No, I'm afraid not. Now I'm too busy with other things."

Sally seemed to put on her most flirtatious

little-girl manners whenever she was introduced to a male friend of her mother's, and it sometimes embarrassed Felicia. But now, watching Sally rotate her body, hands clasped behind her, eyes opened wide with precocious eyelash batting, Felicia was horrified to hear her make pronounced hints.

"I wish Mr. Mitchell could teach me, just like he did you, Mommy. I wish I could take a lesson from Mr. Mitchell. I never had a real ski coach."

Grant and Felicia couldn't hide their smiles at Sally's exaggerated self-pity. Then Felicia told her daughter, "You're not quite ready for coaching; you have some fundamentals to learn first. Now come along and let's find our equipment."

Felicia could feel resistance as she pulled Sally along. The child walked forward, but kept her head turned to the back, and her gaze fastened with unconcealed fascination upon the man following them. Felicia prayed that her child wouldn't become difficult and openly pout over the rebuff she'd received at her idea, so she quickly cast about for a distraction.

"You'll have to unlock your own skis from the rack. Show Mr. Mitchell how you've learned to do that."

The ploy worked, and Sally sprang forward to go to work on her equipment. As Felicia began to unfasten her own skis, she was startled to find a gloved hand placed over her own, stopping her.

"May I make a suggestion?" Grant said, leaning close to her ear. "A parent is the worst possible teacher for his own child, don't you know that? It's like a man trying to teach his wife how to drive. You're too emotionally involved with your student. You might spoil skiing for Sally if that happens."

Felicia turned to look at him, knowing he was right.

He held the ends of first one glove and then the other in his teeth as he pulled them off, then reached out to take her ski hat in both of his hands. He gave it a pull this way and then that until he was satisfied that it was resting straight on her head.

"I think we should do just as your smart little girl suggested. Let me teach her."

"You want to give her a lesson?" she asked him, unfortunately in a voice louder than his so that Sally, now approaching them with her skis thrown over her shoulder exactly as Grant had carried his, heard her.

"Oh, Mommy, is he going to teach me

84

after all? Am I going to have my very own coach?"

Sometimes Felicia almost burst out laughing at her daughter's melodramatic techniques for getting her own way. But at this moment she was confronted not just with Sally's insistence, but with Grant's as well, for he had reached out already to take the little girl's hand, and Sally looked completely bewitched, ready to follow him up any yellow brick road.

"Come on, little thing. Let's see if we can make you a racer. Tell me, what did they teach you yesterday?" he asked her.

"They taught us how to get on the chair lift."

"Oh, good," he laughed. "Now if we can teach you how to get off, you'll be more expert than your mother by this afternoon."

"See you later, Mom," Sally said with an arrogant little twitch to her bottom as she looked over her shoulder. How proud she was to have gotten her own way, and the chance to spend time with this intriguing stranger. Grant turned back then to give Felicia an okay sign with his fingers to assure her that her presence with them was unnecessary.

With the greatest effort at restraint Felicia watched them walk off together toward the bus loading area, and then she turned back toward the lodge. She planned to have one more cup of coffee and then head to the opposite end of the valley to ski Baldy. If she skied hard enough, she might be able to keep her mind off of the fact that Grant and Sally were together for the very first time.

By two o'clock that afternoon Felicia was sitting on the outside deck of the hut at the base of Half Dollar nursing along a cooling hot chocolate and watching the classes of beginners bump and roll about on the low rise of the mountain. She had spotted Grant and Sally a few moments before getting onto the chair lift, and now she waited expectantly to see how the pair would get down the hill.

Grant was bound to be impressed by what a four-year-old child could do, not knowing that she was older than he thought. Felicia just hoped that the subject of birthdays wouldn't happen to come up. Luckily Sally still couldn't recite the months of the year in order, and often placed her birthday month of March right before Christmas, so maybe if they happened to discuss it, Grant would end up as confused as Sally. Letting them spend time alone together was a risk she hadn't planned to take, but it had been unavoidable, and now she counted on the fact that the encounter would probably leave Grant bored and uninterested.

After all, what further thought would a man like Grant give to a child? He had never been interested in children, never wanted any of his own. They certainly didn't fit in with his pattern of living. He was only curious to see if he could discover a spark of talent, the promise of a future Olympian, in Felicia's offspring. There was no chance that the significance of this day would ever be suspected by Grant Mitchell.

It was never hard to spot the graceful dark question mark of Grant's body over his skis even from far below him on the hill, and now there was a tiny red spot dotting along behind him. Slowly, slowly, and with overstated precision, Grant executed snowplow turns that seemed in danger of running out of steam from lack of speed. How patient he had to be, inching down the hill in almost perpendicular traverses that looked like the path of a shoelace on a tall hiking boot, his head turned back to call encouragement to the imitator behind him on every turn.

If they'd clear this hill of all the innocents who might be wounded, Grant could come straight down it, flipping from forward to backward, holding one ski in the air, and whooping out the saucy calls of the hot dog skiers he loved to imitate. But today he'd harnessed all that electric energy.

Seeing that they were both smiling when they got to the bottom of the hill, Felicia decided that the day's instructions had gone well, and she went inside to order cocoa for her daughter so it would be hot and waiting and she might be encouraged to rest awhile. When she came back out onto the porch, she stopped stock-still in her tracks as she watched Grant and Sally approaching.

They had removed their skis and spiked them into the snow to stand in wait for their return. Now Grant had Sally lifted up onto one shoulder, and she was grabbing at his hair with one hand, and waving the other in the air pretending to be afraid of losing her balance, but in reality loving every second of his play. But it was their faces, so close together and sharing so similar a mood, that caught Felicia's attention.

Sally's hair was a shade lighter than Grant's and her skin pale and baby soft in contrast to the rough tanned-leather texture of his face. But their expressions were mirror images of one another and the details of their facial structure almost exactly the same, if one stopped to make the study. There was an arch to Sally's upper lip, a flatness to the side planes of her nose, an imperious tilt to the chin, that could only have come as an imprint from Grant's own face. Felicia felt a choking sensation, and she clutched at her throat through the binding collar of the jump suit.

Seeing the face of her husband re-created on the face of their child was a common enough pleasure that women all over the world experienced daily. But until this moment it had been denied her, and the powerful significance of it did not escape her. What was the scientific result of genes and chromosomes mingling and asserting their dominance was also the plain and visible evidence of a love once exchanged, an unbreakable bond once created.

She put the cup down on a redwood picnic table nearby and turned away to compose herself. She could not stand to see them together like this anymore. She'd never considered what agony this secret would cost her if ever father and daughter were brought together. But now, seeing them acting out a vignette that any observer would consider just a small part of a rich family life, she realized how much each had missed in not knowing the other. It made her wish for things that could not be. It made her sorry that Grant Mitchell was not a different sort of man. She was tortured by the same thoughts she'd had during the days late in that awful summer, just before she'd packed her suitcases and taken off in an opposite direction, leaving him for good.

Sally had been only a small bit of tissue inside her at that time. But her presence had been just as much an influence as it was today. It was because these two were incompatible that she'd done it; it was because they would only have hurt each other ultimately; it had been for their own good.

She wiped her eyes on her sleeve, then turned to watch Grant toss Sally onto the ground. He was grasping at his back as if she'd hurt him, and she was laughing at his performance with delight. But such happy moments would have been few no matter what course Felicia had taken all those years ago. The decision had been tough, but she'd made it, and it was irrevocable. Now to be teased and misled by these glimpses of vacation fun was a cruel trick of fate.

Five more days of this! Or however long it was before Grant received a call from

Kitzbühel or Val D'Isere, or Cortina, and had an excuse to plunge back into the more lively waters, back in the stimulating company of his worldly friends.

"Did you see me? Did you see me make the last turn real fast!"

Sally was calling to her from the other side of the railing, and Felicia quickly tried to pull herself together enough to face them.

"It was perfect. Now come and warm up for awhile."

"You should be very proud of your little girl. She's inherited her mother's fine body as well as her winning ways," Grant said to her, clunking the snow off of his ski boots as he crossed the deck.

"You've kept her at it too long. I can see already that she's overtired."

He stopped to give her a probing look that proved she'd caught his attention.

"I don't know much about these things, but she seems fine to me."

"I had planned a much less strenuous day for her, and I really don't appreciate your intruding yourself this way into our plans."

Grant stepped closer to her, obviously startled by her unexpected outburst. "Now, simmer down, sweetness, and tell

91

me what's the matter. What is it that's really bugging you?"

Grant was speaking to her just as he had so many years ago, with the same mocking edge to his words, using the same pet name for her.

"I wanted to ski with my daughter today, and you swept her away from me before I had a chance to complain, that's why I'm angry."

Sally came up to them, unaware of any dissension. "Is this my cocoa, Mama?" When her mother didn't answer, she shrugged and hungrily sat down at the table and started in on the drink anyway.

Felicia's ire was working itself into a full-scale scene as she squared off against her ex-husband.

"It was a stupid idea for you to pretend to be friends with me, and to try to make friends with my child."

Grant took hold of her stiffened arm and pulled her aside. "I had no idea that I would be upsetting you so. There doesn't seem to be much that I do or say that pleases you."

"That's right! You never think about what other people want. You are a thoughtless man, always trying to have your own way. You're pushy, and you're arrogant, and . . ."

Grant's reaction to her stormy words was just what it had always been. He kept his voice calm and quiet, but his eyes hardened into cold pools of frozen anger. His temper was more suppressed and therefore more awesome than Felicia's blustering name calling.

"The years have been good to you, Felicia. You're more beautiful than ever, and you're still a gorgeous sight to see on skis. But I thought that by now you would have learned to control that temper. I was hoping that the years had brought you some maturity."

Felicia realized her attack might have hurt him, and she regretted it already. "I'm sorry; it's just that . . ."

"You'll have to control that cutting tongue of yours and stop acting childish. I've invited your daughter to dinner tonight."

"You've what?"

"I promised her beef fondue in the Ram if she'd keep her weight on that downhill ski. And, of course, like a little trooper, she did."

"You shouldn't have made her a promise that you couldn't keep. You have no idea how and when children eat. And besides, we have other plans, we're meeting friends . . ."

"As opposed to ex-husbands, is that it?"

He stared at her a moment more, then turned to Sally.

"Good-bye, Sally. I'll see you tomorrow."

"Oh boy, another lesson, Mr. Mitchell?"

Grant gave Felicia a quick look, then knelt beside the table so that he could look straight at Sally. "You don't need any more lessons. Just practice with your mother tomorrow what I taught you, okay? And we'll have that dinner some night later this week."

"All right, coach. Can I have another cocoa, Mother?"

Grant unzipped his pocket and found a quarter. "Here you go, flash. Stoke up that energy."

"She's a marvel," he sighed as Sally scampered inside. "I didn't realize kids had so much go-power. It's a shame her father couldn't have seen her today. He would have really had something to brag about."

Felicia turned to look at him with eyes that she knew were overly bright. "Her father sees her. You don't have to pretend sympathy for him."

"I'm sure he does. That's not what I meant. I only thought that it was a shame he couldn't be here to see her on skis. By the way, when the chair lift operator asked Sally her name, she told him it was Sally Hollingsworth."

"Yes?" At first Felicia didn't understand why there was an inquiring look on his face as he leaned back to rest his hips on the table behind him.

"Well, is that her name? I mean, that's your maiden name."

"As I explained, when I work at the ski shop, they want to know me by the name I used when I was competing. So I had to discard my married name." This act was becoming more and more awkward.

"I found that out yesterday from the operator when I placed that call to your room. But doesn't Sally carry her father's name?"

"It just got too complicated, explaining things to the school and to everyone we met. It seemed simpler to change her name to match mine."

"I see."

No, he didn't see at all. There had been no problem with names, for her divorce from him was final and her maiden name returned to her before Sally was born. And there had never been any second husband. If only he knew that the ghostly presence he resented so had never even existed.

He started to say something but seemed to change his mind and instead stood giving her an oddly speculative look that seemed to suggest he was considering her reply with some skepticism. He obviously did not approve. Finally he shook off his censure and started to leave.

"I have some long distance telephone calls to make, so if you'll excuse me . . ."

"Grant?"

"Yes."

"Thank you for teaching her. She'll remember it."

"I hope she will. She has the talent to be a good skier, maybe as good as her mother was."

Felicia watched him go, knowing that this good-bye was more permanent than he could have guessed. Now she was the one who craved a good-bye kiss, for she knew it was possible that the two of them might never see each other again.

During the last few minutes, even during her most antagonistic words, she had come to an important decision. She knew that she had to leave Sun Valley immediately. It meant cutting their vacation short, and probably sacrificing some of the hard-earned money she'd put out in advance, but she could no longer expose herself to the pressuring presence of the man she had once loved with all the fervency of her young emotions. She could no longer be sure of what she might do or say next. The strain of her roller-coaster memories, shooting her from the highs to the lows as she remembered her days with Grant, was twisting her nerves into shredded cables in danger of breaking. She was going to run away from him again.

When Sally returned from the cafeteria line, Felicia began to lay the groundwork.

"How would you like to go to Disneyland, Sally?"

"How can we do that? Disneyland is back home in California. We're in Idaho, aren't we, Mommy?"

"Well, we're going back home to California."

"Today?"

"Maybe. If I can arrange things. Hurry and drink that up so that we can get back to the lodge."

The manager was cooperative when Felicia explained that there had been an emergency in her family and she had to return home unexpectedly. Sally was less accommodating, and fired questions and complaints throughout the packing process. But she soon noted her mother's thin-lipped insistence, and, realizing even at her age the futility of one stubborn Scandinavian trying to change the course of another, she abandoned the struggle.

★ ★ ★

On Monday morning when Felicia walked in the back door of Fun Sports, her friend Nadine met her in the coffee room with hot cinnamon rolls and consolation.

"Are you just returning from vacation, or from prison? You look awful!"

"It wasn't my all-time favorite ski trip. Is Dan in yet?"

"Not yet, so relax and have one of these."

"Those smell yummy. Did you just bake them this morning?"

"Yes, and you look like you need one. I wish I could come back from a vacation looking as thin and wan as you look! I always come back looking like Heidi after she ate her way through the Alps."

Felicia went to put her arm around the chubby shoulders of her best friend. "Well, you're a beautiful sight to me, Nadine."

"Now, tell me what went wrong on your trip."

Felicia heard the roar of the manager's sports car in the back parking lot. "It's a long story, and there isn't time right now. Come home with me tonight for dinner and we'll talk."

"If you've got any meat at your house, I'll make us some goulash. I'm hungry for something with noodles." Nadine licked her lips in anticipation.

"You're determined to fatten me up, aren't you?" Felicia asked her with a laugh, but the merry sweep of her lips dropped away as soon as the door opened and Dan Fowler walked in.

"Hello, beautiful. Come back to me at last?"

"Good morning, Dan," Felicia tried to be pleasant.

"Don't you have books to keep, Betty Crocker?" Dan snarled at Nadine, grabbing the last roll from her fingers and pushing it into his own mouth. "Pour me some coffee, Felicia," he said as he chewed.

Nadine gave Felicia a "here we go again" Monday smile, and headed for the door. Before leaving the room, she received one of Dan's gratuitous pats on the tautly stretched backside of her slacks.

"Swing it, baby. You've got a lot to swing," he taunted, and Nadine's cheeks turned bright red. She didn't get many passes from men, and when she got them from him, Felicia could tell it hurt her deeply to realize it was only done to make her appear foolish.

With Felicia, his passes were more serious. As soon as Nadine had left the room, he came to stand behind her at the coffee cart, his body obscenely pressed against hers. She tried to pour coffee as he pawed her shoulders roughly.

"Please, Dan. You asked for coffee and now you're making me spill it."

"Ah, come on, sweetheart. I'm going to give you the welcome home you deserve."

"Here, drink your coffee. You look like you could use it."

Dan's face was prematurely lined, and his eyes baggy from too many nights spent at activities more rigorous than mere sleep. He took the cup and with his other hand pushed his hair back off his sleepy face.

"Boy, you're right. I need this. You should have seen the chick that followed me home from here Friday night. I've been fighting her off all weekend."

"I can see that a lot of stock has come in while I've been gone, so I'd better get busy unpacking and marking it."

"Just a minute." Dan put down his cup and followed her into the storeroom. "You haven't shown me how you missed me."

Felicia took a big sigh, realizing she should never have let him get her into the dim room with only one door. She'd been gone just long enough to forget all her old avoidance tactics.

She leaned away from him toward a shelf to grab up a handful of labels, and Dan took hold of her and twisted her toward him. He lunged at her, trying to kiss her, but she pulled away, lifting her head just in time for his mouth to catch her squarely on the chin rather than on the lips. She heard him gasp angrily and prepare for another approach, and this time she waited in stony rigidity. As his kiss connected properly this time, she was reminded of Grant's last kiss. She closed her eyes, pretending she was still in Sun Valley, and pretending that Grant was pursuing her lips, this time not in anger but with real desire for her. But the trick didn't work, for Dan's kiss was boorish and crude, with none of the provocative allure that Grant had always been able to seduce her with in the old days.

Dan, for the moment at least, seemed satisfied.

"Now, then. I'll let you get to work. But that was only a reminder of what's to come. I haven't given up on you yet, Felicia." He left to retrieve his coffee cup and go to the front of the store to open up for the day.

Felicia went out into the hall, shaken by the awful reminder of what her working days had been like since Dan took over as manager. She leaned into the tiny cubicle where Nadine was bent over her ledgers, her fingers moving up and down the keys of the ever-clattering adding machine beside her.

"I don't know how much more of this I can stand, Nadine," she groaned.

"Well, it's a living. It pays the bills. Just remember that."

"There must be a better way."

"When you find it, let me know."

The day seemed endless as Felicia constantly devised fancy footwork to keep herself out of Dan's reach. But at last it was closing time, and Felicia locked the doors and turned out the lights. Nadine was dawdling over her work in her office, conscious as always of her promise to remain in the store as long as Felicia was there, to protect her from Dan.

"Good night, Dan, see you in the morning," Felicia called, barely stopping at his office door.

"There's something a couple usually does before they say good night," Dan said, standing up from his desk and coming toward her. He pulled her into his office.

"Dan, don't," she cried out.

"Look, I'm the boss around here."

He slammed the door closed with his foot.

"Please leave me alone. I just want to do my job and . . ."

"Yeah, I know. Do your job and collect your paycheck and then go home and dream your little dreams all alone. What's the matter with you, Felicia? It's time you drop that Ice Queen image of yours and have a little fun. I'm tired of waiting around for you, sweetheart."

He made the term of endearment sound insulting. He grabbed her shoulders roughly, pulling her silky shirt-blouse into disarray, and she could feel his steamy breath, unpleasant on her neck.

"Get your hands off of me. I'm not merchandise, and don't act as if I belong to you." She blew the warning draft into her bangs, surprised by her new burst of confidence in standing up to him when she'd kept her temper under wraps for so long.

"As long as I sign your paycheck, you do."

"Well, if that's true, then I don't want any more of your paychecks."

"You have a child to support, don't forget. You need this job and you need what comes with it — me!"

Felicia took a deep breath, as if she were pushing herself downhill over the cornice.

How good it felt to release the contempt that she'd had to keep from him for so long!

"You are a repulsive, lecherous idiot, and you have taken advantage of me long enough with your clumsy attempts at seduction."

She remembered how Grant had called her tantrums of name-calling immature, and perhaps he was right, for at the moment she felt like an outraged child, and she was barely able to resist the impulse to stick her tongue out at the startled man who was groping at the desk behind him for support.

"You are an arrogant beast, a cheap imitation of a real man, a . . . a . . ."

"He's a slob, don't forget that!" Nadine chimed in from just behind her, and Felicia realized for the first time that her voice had been raised so loudly in anger that her friend had come running to join in the fun.

Dan's face was white with rage. "I hope you two realize what you're asking for. I'm calling the owner. I'm going to tell him you both are fired."

"That's fine with us," Nadine charged, and Felicia felt the adrenaline flowing through her body just as if she were finishing in a race to the wire.

Before either one of them had time to consider the consequences of what they'd just done, they were out the door. Felicia

104

picked up Sally at the daycare center, then trudged up the steps to her apartment door, carrying the depressing stack of bills that she'd just found in her mailbox. Nadine had let herself in with the extra key she carried and already had something going on Felicia's stove.

After giving Sally a big welcome-home hug, Nadine said to her, "Your mother and I have had a terrible day. Can you find some coloring to do in your room while we have a glass of wine and try to figure out how to repair our lives?"

"Sure, Nadine. Mommy has her sad face on. I hope you can make her smile like you always do."

Felicia took a glass of wine and sat down on the couch, putting her feet up on the battered coffee table in front of her.

"Well, what are we going to do?" she asked her friend after her child had left the room. "I used up most of my savings to take that awful vacation."

"We're going job hunting, that's what."

Felicia raised her glass toward her friend. "Well, here's to poverty." She took a large gulp of the cheap red wine and then looked over at the stack of mail on the table. One crisp white envelope stood out from all the others. "Hey, this is from Sun

Valley. Maybe that nice manager is sending my refund money already, and we can plan on eating the rest of the week."

"Oh, goodie, goodie. The wolf will stay away from the door," Nadine joked, rubbing her hands together with glee.

When Felicia took a closer look at the envelope, the wan smile fell from her face, for "G. Mitchell" was scrawled in the corner above the smiling sun-face logo of the resort. "My God, it's a letter from Grant."

"Your ex?" Nadine asked.

"Sh," Felicia warned, glancing toward Sally's door. Seeing her shaken expression, Nadine went to close the door.

"What happened? Was Grant in Sun Valley?"

"Yes, he must have written this right after we left."

"Well, open it. Don't just stare at it as if it's booby-trapped."

Felicia slit open the envelope, dreading what might be inside. She read the letter through slowly, trying to absorb its meaning, while Nadine left her alone to go see to their dinner.

Dear Felicia,

Since you left here so abruptly, I didn't

get a chance to continue our conversation about Deer Meadow. I prevailed upon the manager to give me your address, and I hope you won't blame him for this intrusion of mine in writing you directly.

Despite your attitude of bravado and your pretended lack of concern about money, I was able to detect in you a decided interest in making a financial profit from Deer Meadow.

After thinking it over, I've decided that the most advantageous arrangement for you would be to go there, live at Deer Meadow, and develop it yourself into a ski resort. You've kept your connections in the ski world, and I think what you don't know about the resort business you could quickly learn. The potential is there to make a decent living right away, and a tremendous financial windfall after some years of hard work. It would afford you the outdoor life you still seem to enjoy, and would certainly be an ideal country atmosphere in which to raise a child.

As I told you, I harbor some guilt over

our divorce settlement. I feel I owe you some help, and would like to offer it to you in the form of my advice and expertise in your development of Deer Meadow.

I'm leaving tonight for Europe, but should be back in a few weeks. Please wire your decision to my office in New York (address below) so I can begin lining up contractors to do the work you'll need and possible investors to help you finance the improvements.

I'm enclosing a map in case you've forgotten the location of the property you own. If this idea does not interest you, then pardon my presumption in suggesting it. Perhaps your life is too secure, your ties to Southern California too binding, to disrupt.

Sincerely, Grant.

Felicia reread the letter, trying to imagine her former husband's voice saying the words to her. Though he had expressed himself in the straight, logical way of a businessman, he had conveyed a most radical idea, and one that Felicia could not even consider at first. His suggestion that she pull up stakes and go to live in some old place three hundred miles away that she'd only seen from the air seemed like insanity.

"At least you don't look angry," Nadine said, peeking out of the kitchen. "Just numb. Do you want to tell me what's got your mind in such a whirl?"

Felicia threw the letter across to her, not hesitating to share it. Nadine was the one person in the world who knew the complete story of Felicia's past.

Nadine read the letter slowly, her lips moving as silently as a beginning reader's as she mouthed Grant's words.

"Gee, I didn't know you were a big landowner," Nadine giggled as she put down the letter.

"I had forgotten all about it." Felicia shook her head with wonder, realizing just how tumultuous her feelings had been at the time of the divorce.

Felicia sat quietly for a long time, and Nadine sat down with her, careful to say nothing to interrupt her thoughts. At last Felicia spoke, slowly at first, but then gaining momentum.

"What have I got to lose? Do I have a beautiful apartment? Do I have to quit a wonderful job? Is there a line of suitors around the block that I must give up? Will I be losing close contact with a big, supportive family? I don't have any of those things! I have nothing to lose. There's no risk at all to trying this."

"So you're going to do it?" Nadine asked.

"Yes, I am."

Nadine looked at her with wide eyes that seemed melancholy. At last she said, "I'll miss you, Felicia. That's the only thing."

"No, you won't miss me. You're coming along, too. You lost your job out of loyalty to me. Now I'm hiring you. You can cook for us, and keep the books, and work yourself crazy. How's that for an offer?"

"It beats having my bottom pinched by Dan Fowler every day and living in that crummy room at my aunt's house. Oh, Felicia. This is so exciting! Just promise me that I can stay inside bent over the stove, that I never have to step onto skis. You know, I've never been in the snow before."

"You're going to love it, and so is Sally. This is a way to solve all our problems."

"Good-bye San Fernando Valley. Good-bye smog and traffic."

"Deer Meadow, here we come." The two women toasted each other with their glasses, exchanging radiant looks, full of confidence. But after Nadine had left and Felicia was alone without the reinforcing jocularity of her friend, she became unsure of herself. She wandered into Sally's room and looked down at the red-cheeked child who was sleeping on her back with her arms sprawled wide open in confident acceptance of the security of her world. She put one hand down on her daughter's face, automatically monitoring the even breathing of the defenseless child who was in her care.

Oh, Sally, what am I doing? First I let my temper blast forth today so that I lose my job. And now this letter comes and I jump on it like a dog on a bone. How can I be sure what is best for you? What am I doing to your life?

She left the room, wishing she had a snowy field to walk in tonight while she considered this decision she'd made in such haste. It was so hard to decide all alone what was best.

If I go to Deer Meadow, I'll probably see Grant again. We'll have more contact. And that's just what I've always avoided.

Then she stopped pacing and looked around her at the confining four walls of her living room like a crazed prisoner. Her mind was throwing tough questions at her

111

as fast as Sally usually did.

But maybe that's why I'm doing it. Maybe I'm rushing out of here to chase after trouble. After five years of working my head off to do what's right, am I throwing it all away? Am I heading for disaster? Am I really running after Grant?

CHAPTER FIVE

Sally sat in the back seat trying out the pleasures of bubble gum for the first time while Nadine sat in the front seat with the map and helped Felicia navigate. All three were in high spirits as they left Los Angeles the day after the moving van had taken all their worldly possessions ahead of them. Their car was full of singing and joking as they drove north through the Mojave Desert to Bishop, and they spent the night in a motel room, eating take-out chicken from a cardboard box and weaving daydreams about their new life.

"Mommy, are we really going to live in a hotel? Just us, with a whole hotel all to ourselves?"

"It's not really a hotel. It's more like a big house with lots of bedrooms for company to come and stay in. That's called a lodge."

"Oh, like the lodge at Sun Valley, where we stayed?"

"Well, not quite that elegant, yet," Felicia said, her eyes glazed over with visions of what their resort could become, with skiers in fashionable clothes arriving daily with piles of expensive luggage.

The next morning they took up their positions in the car again to start into the Sierra Nevadas. Soon the car heater was running, and they were putting sweaters on as the roadside became first dotted, then banked, with snow.

"According to this map we should turn off pretty soon on the road to Buckskin Village," Nadine said. "That's the nearest town to your place. If we stay on this highway, we'll end up in Clarita Valley. That must be a pretty large town; this shows it has a school, and a church, and a hospital."

Buckskin Village was not so well equipped, having only one gas station, a small general store, and three or four old houses. But under its glamorizing coating of snow it looked like a picture postcard.

"There's a place where we can stock up on food," Nadine said.

While Nadine shopped, Felicia took Sally for a walk through the snow. Beside the tiny parking area, where car tracks had striped mud in a hectic pattern of broken snow, there was an open field of powder snow, unblemished and inviting. Sally stomped and marched and fell over, flapping her arms, as Felicia watched her, her heart brimming over with relief. Above her was blue sky, and all around her was the open feeling of space. This rural atmosphere would bring both of them to bloom, she now felt sure. Their life was going to be full and rich, and they would be together as much as they wanted, romping through the snow, making snowballs, dragging sleds.

When Nadine came out with six or seven bags of groceries, Felicia and her daughter raced each other to the car, their eyes matching in brilliance.

"There's enough food there for a banquet," Felicia laughed.

"We're going to have a feast tonight in our own banquet hall. Should we dress for dinner the first night, do you think?" Nadine asked, pursing her lips, pretending she was on some kind of expensive travel tour.

"Why not?" Felicia played along. "I think I'll wear the blue chiffon."

"I do hope the après-ski activities will be stimulating at this new place. I'm so bored with bridge." Sally laughed at Nadine's la-tee-da voice.

"Do you suppose the earl will be here?" Felicia said.

"Does he care for skiing? I thought it was she-ing he'd taken up this season."

They were all laughing together at their

game as they negotiated the last few turns the map showed them. They were passing through a forest of sugar pines, and they began craning their necks, almost wriggling with excitement, to see who would be the first to spot the Deer Meadow lodge.

"Look at those cliffs just ahead. They must go up about a mile," Nadine said, her face close to the car window, exaggerating the steepness of the area that would someday be groomed and cleared into ski trails.

"The last time I saw that mountain was from the air. The lodge should be right at the base of the hill. It should be . . . Oh, my God! There it is!"

They all stared with disbelief at the dark and forbidding structure just ahead of them. With shutters hanging askew at this angle and that, and with a half-fallen tree leaning against it like a drunk at the bar, the place was a disaster, with an atmosphere that seemed derelict and unwholesome, as if it had been left to rot in its disgrace, unloved in this isolated mountain pass.

"You both stay here in the car a minute," Felicia instructed, trying to keep her voice from wavering. She fumbled in her handbag for the key her brother had sent. She crossed a veranda-like porch where several years' accumulation of blown pine needles and leaves formed mounds of debris under snowy drifts and opened the door like Pandora about to let loose demons from her fateful box.

Huddled in the center of the gloomy, cavernous space she entered was a pathetically small pile of furniture and boxes which the movers had brought the day before. It all looked unusually clean and innocent, and seemed menaced by the surroundings somehow. For, circling the edges of the room, broken or tipped over, were chairs and tables of ancient vintage and no particular style. Dank under their layers of dust, they seemed to be eyeing all newcomers from their shadowy corners, planning ways to frighten them away.

Felicia heard small rustling sounds that frightened her at first, and then she realized that Nadine and Sally were venturing out of the car to follow her, and her heart sank as she waited for them to see this hideous place that they'd all had such high hopes for. She couldn't bear to watch their reaction, and she made her way carefully through the dimness, walking toward the back fireplace wall of the big main room, kicking at pieces of trash and wondering why Grant had ever thought there was any hope of restoring this hopeless wreck.

Damn him, she thought, for building up my hopes, and making me dream about a good future, a happy life here. It was impossible. The place was a ruin.

She heard the wordless moving about of the two who had followed her inside, and their gasps and murmurs as they became aware of the full extent of their plight. She couldn't face them yet, and she went to the big window beside the filthy, charred black hole in the stone wall that had served as a fireplace. She wiped at the dirty glass with her mitten and then peeked through.

Across a wide meadow of snow began a gentle rise, and then the lofty pitch of the beautiful white mountain, glistening in the midday sun. To a skier it was beguiling and it beckoned her to come and explore it. There were rolls and paths of terrain, through groves of pines and patches of snow-covered brush, that offered a multitude of exciting experiences on skis. She could picture where a rope tow would lift the beginners to a gentle place, and where a chair lift could take intermediates on up to the more challenging bowls. She began to see it through Grant's eyes, the eyes of a developer, one who knew how to build and change things and make them better.

"Does this belong to us?" Sally said timidly as she came to stand beside her mother, reaching up to take her hand for reassurance.

And suddenly Felicia remembered that it did. This was hers, it belonged to her, and she could make of it whatever she wanted: a defeat or a victory. And at that moment she decided that she wasn't going to turn away from the challenge. This time she was going to stay in the race.

"Yes, it does belong to us. It isn't much, but it's all ours, and it's all we have."

She turned to face Nadine whose usually cheerful face seemed pale in the ghostly light. Poor Nadine, who had elected to take on this flight of fancy with them. Nadine, who had given up a snug haven in her aunt's home, and a predictable career as a bookkeeper in a bustling city.

"I peeked into the kitchen," Nadine began, but it must have been beyond description, for her words faltered and she did not go on.

"Well," said Felicia, pushing her hair up off of her forehead with the palm of her hand with a gesture of determination, "we have three problems. This place is cold. And this place is dirty. And this place is a mess. Which shall we tackle first?"

"If I get some lights on, and find out how to heat things up, we'll all feel better," Nadine said, beginning to come to life.

"And I think if I find our box of cleaning supplies and get to work on just this one room, we can worry about the rest later," Felicia said, not anxious to look any further for problems.

"Can I help, too?" Sally asked with a spunky voice that made Felicia so proud of her that she could have hugged her. "I'm going to start opening those boxes. I need to find our blankets and our pillows."

And as if all three of them had come to some sort of unspoken agreement that activity and constructive effort might help them forget their disappointment, they began moving about with almost-hysterical energy.

Nadine disappeared through the tall swinging doors on the left side of the room that led to the kitchen, and within a few minutes she'd found the electrical box and pulled some main switch that turned on an old refrigerator and rumbled an unseen furnace into action pushing a rush of air through long unused ducts. Dusty light bulbs here and there even came into brilliance, and Felicia gave a short prayer of thanks that all those mechanical aids were working for the moment, their first stroke of good luck since entering Deer Meadow.

While Nadine went to work putting her groceries away and getting the kitchen organized, Felicia started in cleaning up the filth in the main room. Sally darted here and there all day, righting tables and chairs and helping her mother unpack and arrange things. As evening approached, Sally found some kindling on the front porch and carried it into the stone fireplace; Felicia lit a fire which cheered them immensely.

Suddenly Felicia was tired as she noticed that Sally had curled up with a box of crackers she'd found in one of the cartons and was watching the fire with drowsy eyes. The sounds of mopping and scrubbing had died down in the kitchen, and soon Nadine came in to flop down beside Felicia with a tired sigh on the old couch from her apartment.

"Well, this is a historic day. This is the first time in my life I've been too busy to think about eating. We've missed lunch and dinner."

"I'm sorry, Nadine. I really didn't ever dream it would be like this. We have weeks of hard work ahead of us, if even that will help."

"I'll admit I was scared to death at first.

But when you waded in with such confidence, I just decided to follow after you, and now I'm a believer." Nadine laughed to herself. "We'll have this place ready for the first guest about the time Sally goes off to college. Say, what's that?"

Nadine nodded toward the fireplace, and Felicia noticed some papers propped up on the massive wood beam that served as the mantel.

She got up and went to take the cracker box from Sally's hand, for she had fallen fast asleep. She gave her daughter a kiss, and then pulled a blanket over her, giving her an unspoken promise that the days ahead would be more secure and organized than today had been for her. Would there ever be time for all that recreation together that she'd dreamed about as they enjoyed the snow earlier? Probably not for a long time. She and her child would have to learn to enjoy the companionship of working together, as they had today, instead.

She reached up to take the folded paper off the mantel, shuddering as she noticed the baleful stare from a deer head mounted above it high on the stone wall.

"The movers must have left their bill here," she said, tossing it toward Nadine. "You're our business manager; you take care of this," she joked.

"It's their bill, all right, but there's something folded inside. Someone has written on it: 'This came while we were unloading the van.' It's a telegram for you."

Felicia opened the yellow envelope with curiosity. The message was short:

HELP IS COMING. WILL ARRIVE
THE 16TH. GRANT.

When she read it out loud, Nadine jumped up and began exclaiming dramatically, "That's just a week away! Our first guest is coming and we aren't ready! What are we going to do?"

"Now stop trying to be funny. He's not a guest, but he is someone we have to impress. If we want to stay here and turn this into a first-class resort hotel, we'll have to convince him that it's savable."

In the morning, when the sun streamed right across the snowy meadow behind the lodge and into the tall besmirched windows on each side of the fireplace, the room seemed even more dingy than it had the day before. But when Felicia awakened, she smelled bacon cooking, coffee brewing, and she could feel the rejuvenation in her body from a good night's sleep on her own mattress which she'd put on the floor in front of the fireplace. She followed her nose to the kitchen.

It was a huge room, adjacent to the main reception room and almost the same size and shape, with the cooking area at one end and a row of high windows facing out to the mountain at the other end. Sun was streaming through those windows now, but only served to reveal the dismal effect of years of smoke and grease upon the pitiful room. Though the stove was an old white porcelain monstrosity, Nadine seemed to have mastered it.

They ate in front of the fireplace, and Nadine and Felicia spent the precious moments of relaxation over their meal planning their schedule for the week.

"If we could just get a coat of paint on that kitchen . . ."

"We have to get a phone in. Remind me when I go to town to call . . ."

"And we have to wash these windows . . ."

"Before Grant gets here, I want . . ."

Sally interrupted, having caught something of interest in the practical details to which she'd paid little attention until now. "Who's coming? Did you say someone is coming here to stay with us?"

Felicia hesitated a moment, wondering

how she would explain all this. "Yes, dear, Mr. Mitchell. Remember we met him in Sun Valley?"

"My ski teacher is coming to see me?" the little girl asked, her brown eyes dancing with excitement.

Felicia smiled lovingly. The child was flattered that the man she had liked was coming all this way just to see her, and never questioned the logic of it.

"If we're going to be ready for him, we'd better start right now," Felicia said, taking a last gulp of coffee. "The first thing I'm going to do is take down that awful old deer head and lock it away in the basement, if there is one."

"I'm going 'sploring. Is that all right, Mommy? There's rooms and rooms and rooms in this place. Can I pick one to be my room?"

"Of course, darling," Felicia said, stepping onto a chair to begin her project.

Felicia indeed found a doorway leading to a steep stairway into the basement. Juggling the hairy hunting trophy in her hands, she made her way down there and dropped the thing with a cloud of dust onto the floor. She found a light switch, and after flipping it on yelled out with a whoop for Nadine to come and see the

125

treasure trove she'd found. The basement was jammed with furniture, carefully stacked and covered, and Felicia could quickly see that the old leather sofas and heavy wooden tables would serve quite adequately to furnish the big room upstairs.

While she and Nadine were in the basement rummaging happily through the crates of linens and cartons of dishware and pulling dust covers off the furniture, they heard Sally call them and they rushed upstairs. The child had gone through the door directly across the main room from the kitchen entrance. It led into a long hall, and on each side of it were doors into bedrooms. She was running from one to another, and the two women followed her. It was like a game to Sally, but to the others it was the high excitement of relief, for every guest room, though dusty and undecorated, contained sturdy, rustic furniture. There would be no need to make expensive purchases of furniture before these rooms could be inhabited.

Now that they'd begun their exploring, they couldn't stop. They'd all been curious about the stairs in the corner of the main room. They were just to the right of the big front door, and they headed straight upward along the side wall of the room to a tiny landing and a closed door barely visible in the murky darkness next to the heavy crossbeams of the high ceiling.

The door opened into a hall just like the one below it that served the guest rooms, only up here there were just four rooms, large and unfurnished, each with a private bath. These had no doubt served as the owner's apartments.

"I'm going into town and see if I can scare up some helpers," Felicia said, heading downstairs to find her car keys, now charged up with enthusiasm.

The man at the gas station knew of two dollar-poor ski bums in need of some lift-ticket money, and before long she'd found Jeff and Andy and brought them back. They threw their sleeping bags into one of the guest rooms and after the first meal Nadine served them, decided to stay all week.

The boys moved all of the furniture that had come up from Los Angeles into the upstairs rooms, then brought the basement furniture into the reception room. Felicia made a trip to the paint store in Clarita Valley and picked out a beautiful shade of French blue, and the boys painted the kitchen and it brightened up immediately. She had them bring in one of the huge trestle tables and set it up at the end of the room near the windows. Until they could add on a dining room, their guests would have to eat in the kitchen and listen to Nadine laugh at her own wisecracks as she worked.

Felicia, with her long hair pulled into a ponytail, worked all week at window washing and bathtub scrubbing, and slalomed through miles of vacuuming. Once the boys had set up her record rack and her hi-fi equipment in the main lounge, she worked to the music of the London Symphony and found the drudgery more pleasant.

When the sixteenth finally dawned, and Felicia knew that Grant would be there within hours, she fussed over her checklist, hoping they'd accomplished all the modest goals they'd set for themselves.

"Thank you, Jeff, for all the hard work you and Andy have done," she said, handing him a check.

"Just promise me one thing," he said, throwing his bedroll over his shoulder. "I want first chance at a ski instructor job at Deer Meadow someday."

As they watched their helpers leave, Nadine said, "I hope Grant gets here by dinnertime. I have an unbelievable meal planned."

"I'm sure he'll be here by then," Felicia answered. "Now, Sally, why don't you go out and gather up a lot of pine branches, and we'll decorate every bare corner with them? That will bring that delicious smell of the forest inside, just like Christmas."

"Now that you've settled her down, what are you going to do to keep your nerves in control today?" Nadine asked.

"I'm going to add all those final little touches I haven't had time for until now. You know, putting pictures up, stacking books around, unpacking lamps and ashtrays and things."

By four o'clock there was still no sign of Grant, and Felicia had done everything she could think of to dress up the place. So she went upstairs to take a long hot bath and then she dressed for the first time in a week in something besides her work clothes. She put on a quilted skirt in a provincial pattern of browns and beiges, and wore the matching vest over her old reliable cashmere sweater. She heard a car crunching through the snow of the front driveway as she finished her dressing, and in spite of her self-assurances that this day had no personal significance for her, she felt a stir in her blood at the thought of seeing Grant again.

She paused in the darkness of the

shadows on the landing, so that Grant did not notice her when he came in the front door. He shook the snow from his coat, and she watched him from above, hoping to catch his first reaction to Deer Meadow before he saw her.

She knew as she glanced around that he couldn't help but feel drawn into the place. Four huge logs were stacked and blazing in the fireplace, the hi-fi was softly putting forth Smetana's "The Moldau," the smell of a beef roast and Yorkshire pudding came from the kitchen, and the leather couches and dark mahogany library tables were shining from the freshly applied cleaners and waxes.

Grant hung his coat on a row of hooks by the door and then turned around to look over the room, pulling the sleeves of his brown corduroy jacket into place and adjusting the collar of his cream-colored silk shirt. He looked tired after his hours of travel, and Felicia felt a pull of sympathy as she noticed again the deepened creases of his face which added a more austere quality to the carved masculinity of his face.

Just as Felicia began down the stairs to greet him, and solicit his praise for her efforts on the place, she saw the door open behind Grant, and a tall woman in a large furry hat entered the room. Apparently she'd been on the porch drawing off her heavy snow boots, for she was carrying them in one hand.

"Grant, take these!" she ordered, thrusting her boots at him and looking around with a scowl. "If I'd known it was like this, I wouldn't have bothered to remove them."

"Hello, Felicia. Sorry we're so late. But we've had a long trip," Grant said as Felicia came down the steps toward him.

"All the way from Saint Moritz, to this!" the woman beside him said with an obviously critical tone.

"Oh, excuse me, this is Ilse Ruller, an associate of mine. Meet Felicia Hollingsworth, and this is her daughter Sally."

Felicia turned to see her daughter peeking over the back of one of the large sofas from where she was kneeling in hiding, suddenly coy and shy after asking all day when Mr. Mitchell would arrive. At Grant's greeting she slid off the leather and disappeared into the kitchen without a word.

"What a rude child. In Germany we send those kind to bed without their supper," Miss Ruller said, pulling off the furry toque, freeing an impressive fall of thick brown hair that reached almost to her waist. She shook her head back and forth to adjust her hair, then marched off uninvited to begin a tour of the room.

"It is worse than we imagined, Grant, don't you think?"

While Ilse passed judgment on the lounge, Grant pushed open the door into the kitchen.

"And who is this making magic over the stove?" he asked.

"Pulling a cake from the oven is as easy as pulling a rabbit out of a hat," Nadine answered, turning around to dust flour from her hands.

Felicia made introductions all around, and then suggested Nadine come and join them in the lounge for cocktails. She brought in the liquor tray to the low table in front of the fire, and Grant mixed the drinks, acting more the host than the guest.

Ilse began a critical appraisal of what she'd seen of the lodge so far, without being asked for it by anyone. Grant raised one hand to interrupt her, perhaps noticing the offended expression on Felicia's face.

"I told you in my telegram that I was bringing help, Felicia. I can only stay a few days, there are some problems with my place in Switzerland, but Ilse will stay just as long as you need her."

Felicia wrinkled her nose almost imperceptibly as she gave Nadine a look.

"She's run some of the most profitable ski resorts in the world, and she'll show you how to set up your books and run a good reservation system."

Felicia saw Nadine's mouth drop open.

"And," Grant continued, "she'll give you advice on how to plan your advertising, run your dining room, anything like that."

"She's a regular one-woman hotel school," Nadine commented quietly, but Felicia understood the sarcastic message of her words.

"If you'll excuse me, I have to put my little girl to bed," Felicia said, and she went to call Sally and take her upstairs, glad for the excuse to get away from the overbearing woman who had again launched into her blunt critique.

"Eventually, I think this building should be razed. What do you think, Grant? No point in investing much in improvements. The base lodge should be built . . ."

When Felicia came back downstairs, Nadine had disappeared into the kitchen, and Ilse was talking on as Grant stood in front of the fire. He was looking around the room, obviously considering her opinions about the place. When he caught sight of Felicia, his eyes narrowed in deep concentration, and she wondered if he was thinking about the mess he'd gotten her into with his suggestion that she come here. After more than a week of back-breaking work, this so-called expert he'd brought with him wanted to burn down the place!

The dinner was delicious, but Felicia's head began to throb from the loud and constant conversation that Ilse contributed. As soon as the meal was over, she offered to show them to their rooms. Grant brought in the luggage, and she led him to a room with a view of the mountain, while Ilse busied herself opening doors, inspecting every room on the corridor.

"Right in here, Grant," Felicia gestured.

He put his suitcase down and turned to face her.

"You haven't said a word about what you think of the place," she said pointedly.

"I'm still weighing things, trying to make up my mind," he said, coming disturbingly close to her. "The place has charm. But maybe that's just because of all the nice touches you've added."

His words warmed her. That was all she needed, just acknowledgment from him that she'd contributed something during this agonizing week of effort. She looked up at him, feeling his eyes pull hers toward him with their special power to captivate.

"Do you think now that we were insane to buy this without even looking at it from the ground?" she asked him.

"It was the mountain we were buying, and a dream for the future. The mountain is still here, and it's just as magnificent as ever. And the dream, well, it's yours alone now."

The rumble of his voice held her tied close to him, and she watched with fascination as his amber eyes darkened, the pupils dilating into expanding circles.

"I'm glad you decided not to sell this property, no matter what you had to sacrifice in order to come here," he continued, putting his hands on her shoulders. "This is all that's left, the only tangible evidence of that idealistic youth we shared. You're the proper caretaker. Perhaps there's more sentiment in your heart than you're willing to admit, sweetness. Or else why would you be here?"

She couldn't tell him that she was here because she had nowhere else to go. If he wanted to believe that it was her loyalty to the past that had drawn her to this lonely pass in the Sierras, she'd have to let him. But what had brought him here? Before she had time to consider that nagging question any further, she heard Ilse coming toward them with heavy footsteps, and she pulled away so that the curiosity of Grant's employee would not be aroused by the mesmerized way the two of them were locked together by their eyes.

"I don't care for the room where you've put my things. Is there another that's clean enough to sleep in? What about this one right across the hall from Grant's?" Ilse asked.

Felicia hurried over to open up that room, noticing that in testimony to the callouses on her hands, it was as spotless as all the others. Ilse followed her inside and closed the door behind them.

"I'll just open this heater vent. I didn't warm up any other room because I didn't know there was a guest coming with my . . . I mean, with Grant."

"You started to say with your husband, did you not? Old habits die hard, I see."

"He's told you about our . . . situation?" Felicia felt her privacy violated, and she wondered just how casually Grant discussed their personal story with others.

"I was there when it all happened, when he found that letter saying you weren't coming to Europe to join him."

Felicia's shocked reaction seemed to please Ilse. "He was staying at the hotel where I worked in Germany. If you care to know, he spent most of that winter in the bar, drinking away his anger with you. The ski team did badly; they finally went on without him. You managed to stir up quite a lot of trouble."

"That was not my intent," Felicia said quietly.

She was shaken to realize that this woman had had a long and close relationship with Grant. She was not merely a hotel advisor who worked with him. She had been there with him to console him all those years ago.

"I finally taught him to put the past behind him." Ilse was relentlessly continuing. "I showed him how to have fun, let the good times roll, *laissez les bontemps rouler!*"

Felicia stopped, her hand gripping the doorknob to stop it from shaking, and felt as if a ski pole had been jabbed into her heart. That voice, unexpectedly speaking that language, was distressingly familiar. It echoed through her memory, even though it had been a long time since she had last heard it.

"You speak French?" she asked, already certain of the answer.

Ilse stood up straighter, prouder looking, if that were possible. "Of course. My mother was Swiss. I grew up speaking three languages: German, English, and French. You Americans are always so impressed by anyone who knows languages," she said with a disparaging sniff.

Felicia leaned back against the door as a wave of nausea swept over her. A sour, bitter taste came to her mouth as she remembered that day in Portillo, Chile.

She'd returned from her visit to the doctor in a daze, and finding Grant on the phone, she had gone into the next room to think out her dilemma. Finally she had built up her courage, decided to tell Grant what she'd just learned. She picked up the telephone extension to see if he was still busy, and hearing a woman's voice on the line, she'd kept the receiver up a moment longer. The voice had been crooning in French, and though Felicia did not understand the words exactly, she had known they were words of love.

"Mon amour, je t'aime."

In that moment she had decided she must set Grant free. He was not a man who could be tied down, kept in one place, bound to a family. In fact, he could not even remain bound to one woman.

And now she knew that the woman with whom he had been sharing words of love on the long distance line all those years ago, while she stood in the other room feeling her life crack off like an avalanche into a tumble of chaos, had been Ilse Ruller, the woman who was still with him today.

CHAPTER SIX

The low, grating sounds of a conversation full of suppressed hostility came from the kitchen where Ilse and Nadine were squared off across the table from one another, supposedly discussing the proper way to plan ski lodge menus. And at the front door Felicia stood arguing with her daughter.

"I want to go outside."

"But you just came in from playing in the snow."

"Well, I want to go out again."

"I just took off all your outside clothes."

"There's nothing to do in here. I was going to help Nadine make muffins, but that lady came in and told me to go away."

"I'll tell you what. You and I are going to take a little drive together into Clarita Valley." Felicia was just as restless as her daughter and anxious to be away from the tensions at Deer Meadow.

"Where are we going, Mommy?" Sally asked as her mother zipped her into her best parka and slipped her boots onto her feet.

"There's a wonderful school in town,

and we're going to go there and meet the principal."

"Why, Mommy?"

"Because you're bored, and you need to meet some children your age."

When Sally said nothing by way of protest, Felicia knew she'd made the right decision. And when they got to the school office, Felicia learned that Sally was the right age to start a pre-kindergarten program; in fact, she could begin that very day. Felicia filled in some forms, learned about the school-bus schedule, and then watched her daughter walk off with the principal to meet her new teacher with a happy, expectant expression and nary a look back at her mother.

When she returned to the lodge, she still wasn't ready to go inside and listen to Ilse, so she walked around the side of the building and then looked across the meadow. In the winter it looked like a flat saucer of milk placed before the mountainous white cat crouched behind it. Suddenly she noticed that Grant was coming toward her, returning from a walk. She tried to back away before he spotted her, but she couldn't move fast in the deep snow, and he saw her and made a waving motion for her to wait for him.

He was wearing a sleeveless down-filled vest of dark blue over his usual black sweater, and he was thrashing through the snow with exuberance.

"I had an urge to go exploring this morning," he said when he came to her side. "I wanted to figure out some cross-country ski trails. That sport is the big craze lately." He began to walk her back to the lodge, describing his plans, and she noticed as they walked how his arm shot out to grab her when her boot broke through some crust of snow or she floundered in a particularly deep drift. But he seemed to make these tender gestures rather mindlessly, for his attention was focused on their common project, the development of a ski resort.

Felicia wondered as she walked with him whether things would have been different if Ilse Ruller had never come into their lives. Was Ilse a flirtatious home wrecker who had stolen Felicia's husband from her? No, to be realistic, Felicia had to discard that easy cliché. If it had not been Ilse who had driven that final wedge, it would have been Grant himself.

She saw him push a strand of black hair out of his eyes with a characteristic movement of unrest and wondered how much longer he'd remain at Deer Meadow. He'd said only a few days, and she was sure that would be true. His interest span was short, his commitment to any one project was fleeting. He preferred to consult and invest in a variety of resorts all over the world rather than devote his attention to any one of them where he could be owner and manager and enjoy a more stable life.

"Come along with me this way and I'll show you where I think the trails should begin."

"No, Grant. I'm sure Nadine has lunch ready for us by now. We'd better get inside."

Felicia knew she had better not get used to having Grant to guide her through the deep snow.

When they were seated at the table, Nadine asked, "Where did you disappear to, Felicia? Ilse marked you absent at her food and wines class."

She gave Felicia a beseeching look that indicated she had needed her support in facing their common enemy.

"I decided to get Sally enrolled in school."

Ilse put down her soup spoon and looked up with interest. "I didn't realize that in this country they started school so young," she said.

Felicia felt as if twenty people were watching her, instead of just the three. "Well, she's such a bright little girl, and she's had so much nursery school while I've been working, that I felt she was ready for a pre-kindergarten program."

"I had the impression you just started to work recently, sort of as a hobby," Grant said, lacing his fingers together in front of him like a judge considering testimony.

Feeling somewhat backed into a corner, Felicia blurted further, "I just felt that once I had Sally in school here, I would feel committed to sticking it out."

Grant's eyes were prying. "You mean, you've had some thoughts of leaving here, of giving up?"

Nadine interjected, "You didn't see this place when we arrived. It looked like Dracula's guest house. I think if either one of us had had a job to go back to or a dime in the bank, we would have run out the door as if the Count himself was at our heels."

Grant was looking from Nadine to Felicia as if to confirm the dire picture that had just been painted of their financial woes. He leaned on the table, his long body tensed as if he wanted to spring for Felicia's throat himself. Now he knew for sure what he had suspected when he'd seen her all dressed up on vacation and making claims that life was easy and she had been left well taken care of by her second husband. Now that he had confirmation that she had purposely misled him, she was frightened to think that he might pursue the hunt, chasing down all her lies.

"Yes, this place may not impress either of you very much," she laughed with the forced sound of someone trying to seem unworried. "But we've accomplished a lot already. And now we have no intention of leaving."

Dinner that night was a dismal continuation of their previous meals, with Ilse's lectures on hotel management, and Grant's preoccupied absence of attention. As soon as the meal was over, and Felicia had checked that Sally was fast asleep upstairs, she sat down beside the fire and took up her knitting needles to work on a ski sweater she'd begun for her daughter. She could hear Ilse, still droning on in the kitchen, while the long-suffering Nadine accepted her help with the dishes and the boring barrage of words that went with it.

"What a domestic picture you make," Grant said, putting a record on the hi-fi. He came to stand at the end of the couch and watch her, his hands in his pants pockets so that his jacket was pushed back and Felicia's quick glance away from her work took in the lean hardness of his flat stomach beneath his form-fitting turtleneck sweater. He was narrow-waisted beneath broad shoulders that seemed both powerful and graceful. That combination of grace and power was what had made him such a formidable ski racer, and now such an impressive mountain of a man.

Her knitting needles moved faster as she tried to concentrate on her stitches. Knit five, pearl two, knit four, pearl two.

Grant sat down beside her, his arm behind her on the high leather back of the couch. "You seem so different from when we were together. You seem such a homebody. I thought of you then as a girl interested only in the outdoors, in the sports world."

"We found some enjoyment in indoor sports," she said, regretting almost at once her flip joke, for now he was so close to her that she could feel the short gusts of his breath on her hair.

"Yes, we did. There was never any argument in our marriage bed, was there?" He leaned forward to draw back the curtain of her hair, where it was hiding her face from his view as she huddled over her work. He leaned closer to her, to kiss her softly, lingeringly, right on the ear, so that the provocative sound of his lips resounded through her head, and she had to close her eyes to shut off the floodgates of emotion he was unleashing in her. She shook her head slightly to pull her hair from his grasp.

"You can't knit with your eyes closed," he chided, pressing his hand against hers so that she dropped the tangle of yarn into her lap, disregarding the hazard of the stray needles. He lifted his hand then, just far enough to reach the gentle rise of her sweater, where it stretched over her high firm bosom. He rested his hand on her intimately, familiarly, as he had done so often in the golden, sex-hazed days in those chalets in the Alps, and hotels in the Rockies, and rooms in the Sierras.

She leaned her head back and opened her eyes lazily. She was looking up into the dark shadows of the ceiling beams, but she was seeing their bodies intertwined, imagining again that rhythmic ripple of his muscles kneading her to peaks of pleasure she'd never felt since. Behind her the music of Wagner rushed forth into the room, vibrating the air with its rising pulsations, and her breath was coming in time to it.

He must have seen some glowing ember in her eyes that sparked the fire in his own, for he gave a lusty groan that seemed to come from the depths of his soul, and he took her into an embrace that pressed her tightly against his huge chest.

"Let me love you again, Felicia," he said so softly she could hardly be sure of what he'd said. "You have the look of a woman who needs to be loved. A thirsty look you never had when we were together."

Felicia felt the distracting stab of one of the knitting needles in her stomach, but she ignored it as a greater pain took precedence. She felt tears squeeze into her eyes as the truth of his words stirred her first to longing, and then to anger. It was his fault she'd been denied the fulfillment she so craved. If she was parched, it was because he had not been there to quench that craving in her.

"We were always good in bed, Felicia. We always found happiness there," he said.

Inside her she felt a tightening, as if some string that held her together had been wound just a little more snugly around an empty core.

"You found happiness there," she said, forcing the words through her dry lips, wanting to hurt him in her frustration.

"Are you denying that I made you happy?" he said, pulling away from her slightly, his words cooling to room temperature.

"If we'd both been happy, we'd still be together, wouldn't we?" she asked with a purposely nasty jab intended to injure. She wanted to hurt him, to pay him back for the times he'd listened to Ilse's *mon amours,* for the times he'd packed his bags so that she'd had to scurry to pack hers and run behind him to the next stop on the ski circuit, for the last five years of rambling freely over the map while she was alone.

"That's a spiteful thing to imply, Felicia. It makes a lie of all our days together. And most of them were good days."

He stood up and went to warm his back at the fire, one fist clenched and flexing against the palm of his other hand. Felicia felt the chilling premonition that he was planning some sort of revenge upon her, devising a way to make her regret what she'd said. As a husband he had taken great pride in finding new ways to thrill her. Now she was denying those delights, pretending that he had never pleased her with his delicious inventiveness.

She pulled the knitting from her lap with a wincing expression and threw it down on the couch as she stood up. "I'm going upstairs," she said, "where I am not disturbed."

She strode away from him, her hair swinging on each side of her face.

"At least you'll admit I disturbed you," he said with a loud rasp to his voice. "It may have been an unpleasant feeling, but at least you were feeling something."

She could hear Ilse and Nadine coming out of the kitchen, and she hurried on up so that they wouldn't see how he had shaken her composure.

When she got to her room, it was as cold as a lonely mountaintop. She'd opened one of her windows a bit this morning to let in some fresh air and it was stuck in that position. So she undressed quickly and put on her warmest nightgown. It was white flannel with tiny blue nosegays all over it and an edging of blue lace at her neck and wrists. She fastened the streamer of blue satin tightly around her small waist, knowing that with her Alice-in-Wonderland hairstyle she still managed to look as young and virginal as she had on her wedding night. The pregnancy and childbirth, the years of toting a baby on her hip, the hard work and worry of motherhood, had done little to change her appearance. It was inside, where no one could see, that the changes had occurred. Wellsprings had dried up, emotions had stiffened from years of disuse, and even the potent presence of Grant Mitchell couldn't bring her back to those higher planes of feeling that she'd walked on when she was young.

As she huddled under her quilt trying to get warm, she could hear the household quiet down for the night. But she still couldn't relax, and she blamed it on the fiercely cold blast of air coming in her window. She finally got out of bed with an impatient sigh and decided to do something about the problem rather than lie there suffering.

She came quietly down the stairs into the lounge, on her way to the kitchen to find the toolbox. She assumed the room was empty for every light had been turned off, but then she heard the tinkle of ice, and in the fading glow of the firelight she saw Grant sitting alone, a drink in his hands. He was leaning toward the fireplace, staring into the charred remains of the big logs that had blazed there earlier. Now he turned to look at her, and he drew in his breath sharply, as if she had startled him as much as he'd startled her.

Her hand flew to the neck of her gown, and then to readjust the tie at her waist, as she struggled to appear unruffled while explaining herself. "I'm looking for the toolbox. My window won't close and my room is freezing."

Then she realized that her uneasy feeling was caused by the way Grant was brazenly raking her with his eyes, running one hand up and down the frosted glass he was holding as if it were moving over her body.

"I should think you'd like your room as cold as possible. An ice palace for the ice maiden."

She drew her eyes away from his with the greatest effort and went into the kitchen. Even in the dark she went right to the heavy metal box and was stooping to lift it when she felt Grant grasp her from behind. He placed his hands on her waist like a figure skater about to lift his partner into the air and moved her away.

"I'll take care of this," he said, his tone allowing for no argument.

She hurried with quick mincing steps of her cold feet to follow him upstairs to her room. She closed the door behind them so that Sally or Nadine wouldn't hear their voices and be awakened.

Her room was furnished with the things she had bought for her apartment in Los Angeles. All she'd been able to afford were secondhand dressers and chests, but she'd carefully chosen good pieces made of oak, then stripped off the years of varnish and stain and left them plain. Her bed had no headboard, but she'd bought a goose-down quilt of blue velour that served as both bedspread and blankets, and with the blue-and-white-checked sheets and white ruffle-edged pillowcases, it had made even the drab bedroom at her apartment seem warm and homey.

But Grant didn't stop to admire the cozy atmosphere. He spotted the window and went right to work fixing it, whispering swear words to himself as he tried to dislodge it.

"Here, hold this a minute," he said, reaching toward her with a screwdriver.

When she came closer to the window, she could feel again the frigid draft of air, and in spite of herself she shuddered with the cold. Grant stopped what he was doing and looked down at her.

"Here, let me warm you."

There was little passion to his embrace; he simply put his hands on her arms and rubbed up and down briskly so that the friction of his fingers would heat the flannel of her gown. But the impersonal nature of his touch was more irksome than his earlier caresses had been, and she tightened her body into wordless resistance.

"You're as tense and tight as you used to get before a race," he said. And he began to rub her neck and shoulders as automatically as if the old habit had never been curtailed. In a few seconds his massage became less harsh, and his long fingers stretched around her neck with a more gentle pull.

Felicia became aware of the strong scent of liquor on Grant's breath with his face so close to hers, and she wondered how much he'd had to drink while he had sat brooding in front of the fire. She looked up at him with eyes widened by her alarm, studying his face for clues. Even in the cold room there was the ruddy under-coating of a warm flush beneath his skier's tan, bringing vitality and radiance to his face which had seemed so dead and hard just a short time ago when he'd stared at her in the lounge.

She pulled away from his grasp.

"Go get under the covers and warm up," he said, taking the screwdriver from her and turning back to his work.

When he had finished, he walked slowly toward her bed and sat down beside her.

"It's all fixed. The room will warm up in a hurry, now," he said, and she felt the difference already.

They were together in the small circle of yellow light that her bed lamp was giving off. He took her by the shoulders and turned her gently over and began giving her a back rub, still working at the tightness that so afflicted her.

"I remember how to loosen you up," he said as he worked his magic. "I know this body of yours better than you do. I remember all the wires that need to be disconnected, all of the secret places." He spoke rhythmically, in time to the motion of his hands.

She stretched the length of her body, tightening every muscle for just a second, then letting everything go with a sigh. It felt good to be so expertly massaged, and she curled slightly like a contented cat.

"Do you feel warmer now?" he asked.

"Yes," she said drowsily.

"Are you relaxing?"

"Yes, I am," she said, wondering if her voice sounded to him like purring, for it felt that way to her.

"Do you want me to stop?"

"No. I like it. It feels good."

"I can make you feel better."

She rolled over languidly, feeling a slight stirring somewhere deep within her that told her that what he'd done so far was not enough. She was greedy for more, she wanted everything he had to give her.

She looked up into his eyes, and then placed her hands on his shoulders. Was she pulling him down to her, or was he the one who wanted the kiss? She couldn't be sure. But she knew she wasn't resisting him, for her lips parted as soon as she felt his mouth moving gently on hers, and she encouraged his lengthy exploration as he reacquainted himself with the responses of her mouth.

When he pulled back to look at her again, she thought she could see frost melting from the dark depths of his eyes, for bright beams danced in the brown velvet of his eyes, reflecting the lamp beside him.

But then the light went out, and the room was dark. Grant had reached over and pulled the cord on the Tiffany-shaped tulip lamp. She felt the bed sag with the strain of his weight as he stretched out beside her, and she was suddenly confused with mixed feelings. She felt the ache of her need for him, but she was afraid of what might happen if she revisited those hot deserts of desire only he could take her to.

But waves of forgetfulness bathed over her, blessing her with a willingness to suspend reality for the moment, as his experienced hands found those promised places he knew so well. Any misgivings that might have troubled her briefly were soon forgotten.

As he threw back the quilt and began rolling the soft flannel up her long legs, across her hips, and over her head, she moaned her yearnings for him. Just for tonight, let me feel something. Let me be a woman again, she pleaded with him, glad that she didn't have to put her begging into words, for he knew exactly what she sought from him.

Grant made love to her with all the practiced techniques he remembered from their marriage, and her old conditioned responses were intensified by the long years of denial. He seemed determined to make her admit he could please her, and she could no longer hide the fact. Sighs of satisfaction shook through her body as she clung to him, feeling the tingle of reawakening as if parts of her body, long frozen, were thawing out, coming back to life. After the thrilling flights of passion she sank back onto the bed like a bird drifting down into its nest, and she fell into a deep sleep.

She was awakened some time later by soft kisses across her eyes and cheeks.

"Wake up, so I can say good-bye to you," Grant whispered, ruffling the dark brush of his hair against her face.

"Good-bye?" She sat straight up in bed, looking around that dark room trying to remember what city they were in, where he was on his way to, the old anxious feelings coming back to haunt her.

"Go back to sleep now," he soothed. "I just wanted to let you know I'm going back to my room."

"Why, what's wrong?" she asked.

"You don't want someone to find me here in the morning, do you?"

"Oh, no. Of course not." She was grateful for his good sense in thinking of that. Sally sometimes came bursting into her room unannounced, and Felicia wouldn't want her to find Grant there. She could see him getting into his clothes as she sat sleepily pushing her tousled hair out of her eyes and away from her face.

Outside there was a full moon, and it was reflecting off the snowy mountain, giving it a pearly glow that filled the room with a bewitching phosphorescent light. Grant turned to look at her before leaving, and she was conscious of the revealing moonlight upon her bare shoulders and breasts. She started to reach for the comforter to draw it up to cover her nakedness, but his absorbed stare stopped her.

"Now I can see the girl I remember. Open to all the happiness the world has to give her — aglow with the sunshine by day and the moonlight by night."

He came closer to the bed, then sank onto one bent knee beside her. "Keep this blossom open and blooming, Felicia. Don't close off all your chances to live and to feel." Grant was so perceptive, he had felt her numbness give way to feeling, he had known her slumbering emotions were stirred. He let the fingers of one hand trail across her white shoulders. She could sense his hunger for her was just as great as what she felt for him, and she dared to believe during this enchanted moment that the past could be forgotten, that they could return together to that perfect land they'd once inhabited. He kissed her, showing his reluctance to leave, but then left her to sleep.

She awoke in a bed that was still musky with the perfumes of Grant's body. She rolled over onto her stomach, pressing herself against the sheet that was still imbued with his scent, snuggling herself into his side of the bed as if he were still there. She was smiling to herself with the satisfaction of one who has just solved a mystery, or stumbled upon the missing piece to a puzzle. She rolled onto her back again, stretching her arms above her head in sweet lassitude. She hadn't slept so soundly in a long time, and it felt good to come back to earth slowly. But now that she was fully awake, she could sense from the brightness of the day, and the noises downstairs, that she had let the luxury overcome her, and she'd overslept.

She took a bath and put on a warm pink sweater and her ski pants, for no matter what duties awaited her today, she planned to take the time to get outside and enjoy the beauty of Deer Meadow. She realized she had been working too hard lately, spending too much time worrying over the details of setting up the lodge, without stopping to enjoy this beautiful setting. She might just talk Grant into hiking up that mountain with her to do a little skiing, she thought as she glanced outside.

When she came into the kitchen, Nadine had a curious expression on her face as she watched her, humming and smiling, pour herself a cup of coffee from the pot on the stove.

"Hey, Sleeping Beauty. Did you forget we have classes to attend? That Ilse's been looking for you for an hour."

"What time is it? Where's Sally?"

"I got her off to school." To Felicia's worried look Nadine offered quick reassurance. "Yes, she ate her breakfast, and yes, she knew where I had to take her to meet the bus. She jumped aboard as if they were off to the fair."

Ilse burst through the swinging door at that point, her obtrusive commentary already in mid-sentence.

"There are not enough blankets and pillows, and I think the towel count is barely adequate. Felicia, you're going to have to get into that linen closet and check your inventory."

"Good morning, Ilse. Isn't it a beautiful day?" Felicia said. "Why don't we all take a break and get outside and enjoy it."

Ilse stopped to give her the withering look she might give a tardy schoolgirl.

"I was made to understand you wanted to get things in order around here," Ilse said. "Some of us are already hard at work this morning."

Felicia realized then that someone was missing. She tried to make her question sound casual.

"Where's Grant?"

"He was up very early. He went to get estimates from some heavy equipment people in town," Ilse said.

Felicia sat down at the table, and Nadine brought her some corn muffins she'd saved for her from breakfast.

"You hungry?" Nadine asked, and Felicia looked up at the knowing smile on her face that seemed to indicate she could sense something different about Felicia this morning.

The three women spent the rest of the morning at the table, with a few interruptions when Felicia got up to go listen for the sound of Grant's car out in front, or look out the windows at the beckoning hill she was so anxious to explore as soon as a recess was called. But lunchtime came and went and still Ilse talked on, tirelessly going over the reservation forms, stationery, and receipt slips that they must make up for the printer.

They had finished a quick break for soup when Felicia at last heard the sound she had been waiting for, her nerves tightly bundled in her chest with anticipation. She sprang up from the table to go greet Grant at the front door. To her surprise Sally burst in first, and ran to her with a hug.

"My coach came to get me at school, Mommy. Mr. Mitchell came right to the classroom with the principal and found me. All the kids got to see you, didn't they, coach? Tell Mommy."

Grant came slowly in the door behind the little girl, his eyes disappointingly blank as he explained to Felicia, "I was just finishing up my appointments in Clarita Valley when I passed the school, so I thought I'd give Sally a ride home. The principal gave me these for you to fill out. Apparently they're emergency forms or something." He handed her a bundle of papers and then walked off, refusing to meet Felicia's eyes.

The rest of the day went by with no further sign from Grant that the night before had affected him as deeply as it had Felicia. Perhaps, she considered, he was wary of her, fighting his feelings of physical attraction to a woman he'd long ago expunged from his memory. She decided she must give him time to appreciate what had happened between them, to learn to trust her again. He went into his room where he'd had a phone installed, and she didn't interrupt as he kept busy with calls and paper shuffling all afternoon. She took Sally outside with her to review what she'd learned in Sun Valley about the snow-plow stop and the kick turn.

After Sally had been fed, Felicia gave her

a bath and put her to bed, coming to join the others for a drink just before dinner was served. Dinner was a quiet affair, with Felicia still a bit baffled by Grant's subdued mood. He talked little, barely answering her questions about the meetings he'd had that morning.

"I've told you all I know," he grumbled. "I think the local men can do the job, but their prices are going to be much higher than I'd imagined. Just to clear two or three trails this summer will run into many thousands of dollars."

"I don't have that kind of money," Felicia said, her face turning pale as she considered what was ahead.

"And I'm sure you don't want to accept it from me," Grant snapped with such malice in his words that the other two women turned to stare at Felicia to gauge her reaction.

"I didn't know that you were offering," she said, and the looks bounced back to the other end of the table as if the discussion were a tennis match.

"I plan to find you a more disinterested party as a backer," he said. "That way there will be no emotional ties."

Felicia was embarrassed, unable to fathom why his attitude toward her was so disdainful. Did he hate himself so much for giving in to the impulse to make love to her last night? Or was he purposely making her pay penance, hurting her pride as she had once hurt his.

"Excuse me," he said. "I'm going to have some brandy and lose myself in a good book."

As Nadine and Ilse took on their customary chores with the dinner dishes, Felicia followed him into the lounge with slow, dreading steps. Hoping to avoid the confrontation that she could feel simmering to a boil, she decided to go on upstairs and leave him alone.

"Aren't you forgetting something?" he rasped. "Those papers on the table. Sally has to take them back to school tomorrow."

"Oh, yes. I'll take them upstairs and fill them out."

At that moment a burning log fell from the top of its stack in the fireplace, bursting into fiery pieces as it showered the hearth with a noisy explosion of sparks. Felicia jumped as if someone had waved a poker in her face.

"I'd like to talk to you," Grant thundered, and he got up to come toward her. She turned almost as if she were running away from him, and he chased her up the stairs toward her room with the same urgency, slamming her door behind them.

As soon as they were in her room, she knew that something terrible had angered him. This was not merely a dissatisfied lover, grouching over a disappointing night of love. His eyes were like twin fires of rage.

"You are a truly first-class liar, Felicia. You showed off all those fancy clothes in Sun Valley, and assured me you had plenty of money to live on. Then I discover that you've been living like a pauper." He stopped a moment, displaying a glint of ridicule in his eyes. "But you never asked me for any money, did you? Now I know why. After what you'd done, no wonder you felt too guilty to take anything from me."

"What do you mean?"

He grabbed the papers from her hand. "I took a look at these forms the principal gave me. She's already filled in Sally's name, address, and birth date."

Felicia sat down on the edge of the bed, putting her hands up to cover her open mouth.

He waved the papers close to her face. "Now I know the truth about another of your lies. I know exactly when Sally was born, and I know exactly when she was conceived."

Felicia's eyes brimmed with tears when she looked up to watch him striding back and forth, filling her feminine bedroom with his fuming.

"Even with this in my hand it's hard for me to believe it of you, Felicia. I certainly never would have guessed. You had me fooled completely."

"Grant, try to understand."

"No!" He frightened her with his vehemence. "There's no excuse for your deceit. You ruined our lives."

All of Felicia's worst forecasts were coming true. He was reacting just as she had predicted. He considered her pregnancy a betrayal, something she'd done without his counsel and permission, something that had ended their idyllic life together.

But now that he knew, she had to make him see why she'd gone away. She'd done it for him. She'd sacrificed all the happiness she'd known with him so he could go on living the way he wanted, the way he had to live to survive. Being a real husband and a father, tied down to a home, would have killed his spirit, would have made him crazy like a caged animal.

"At least I know now what happened, why you ran out on me," he said with an empty and forlorn sound to his voice that indicated that the knowledge was giving him little comfort.

"Yes, you do. At last we're free of the lie," she said, and he turned to give her a piercing look.

She was relieved that the mythical character and vague excuses would no longer be necessary. Perhaps now, with time, he could come to terms with the truth, have compassion for her motives, and even come to accept his daughter and eventually learn to openly demonstrate some of the fatherly love the child needed.

Grant was rubbing one hand over the rough, shadowed skin of his lower jaw. "I couldn't believe that you'd just send me a letter, tell me you'd fallen in love with another man, and take off that way without giving me a chance to win you back. I would have done anything to keep you, Felicia."

That's exactly why she'd left him in that way. So that he wouldn't try to find her. Once the initial shock of her rejection had died, she had been sure he would be able to forget her, put her out of his mind completely.

"But you couldn't give me that other chance, could you? It was already too late. No reconciliation was possible and you knew it, didn't you?"

She shook her head to try to remove the clouds in her mind. His words had put her in a daze of confusion. He stood over her, his bulk menacing, his face contorted with the ugliness of the accusations he was unleashing on her.

"You were carrying on with that other man and I never even knew it. You were having an affair with him while we were still married. And when you left me, you were already pregnant with that man's child. That's why you left me. I can never forgive you for that!"

CHAPTER SEVEN

Felicia threw herself prone across the bed, sobbing. Grant fell into the rocking chair, his outburst apparently having drained him of long pent-up emotions. She thought the tears would come forever, so complete was her humiliation. How could Grant believe such a thing! How could he come up with such an outrageous conclusion.

But in a few minutes the heaving of her chest slowed to a stop, and she buried her face in the damp quilt, unwilling to face him. She was deeply hurt to think he could believe that she had been a traitor to their marriage. The love she thought she'd seen in his eyes last night had been only her imagination, for now he'd shown what he really thought of her.

"Tell me one thing, Felicia. Tell me who it was. Was he someone I knew? Who were you sneaking off to meet?"

She sat up and stared at him.

"Was he some ski bum or hotel employee in Aspen? Whoever he was, he didn't stay with you long. And he doesn't even bother to support his child. You didn't get much!"

"I have my child," she said dully. "And that's what I wanted."

"Is it? What about having a man around? A real man. Not some sniveling coward who fathers a child by another man's wife then runs away from his responsibilities."

"Don't say any more. I won't listen to your insults."

"You can't stand to hear me attack him, can you? You're still protecting that ex-husband of yours."

"No, I'm not!"

There was no reasoning with him, no way to cut through all his accusations with the truth. She stood up, feeling the ire rising within her. All this absurd jealousy of a man who never existed, it was unbelievable. The unfairness of his accusations, the utter injustice of his condemnation, made her feel like striking out against him. She felt the compulsion to take some physical action, push him from the room, or grab him by the hair and shake the idiocy from his brain.

He must have recognized the aggressive glint in her eyes as she came toward him, for his hands responded quickly, grabbing her to pin her in her place.

"You don't want me to stay again tonight?

You aren't going to invite me into your bed to help you forget the man who got away?"

"How can you say such a thing! What do you think I am?"

"If you could do it last night, you can do it again tonight."

"Get out of here," she shrieked in a voice as strong as a Viking's, and she shook herself free of his grasp with a tremendous surge of indignation.

He left, slamming the door, and she picked up an after-ski boot on the floor and threw it as hard as she could after him to repeat the sound. But during the long cold hours of the night the anger disappeared, and left in its place a spear of sorrow as jagged-edged as an icicle that tore at her heart. She cried and slept intermittently, hating the despair that was replacing that small grain of hope that she'd nurtured in herself since last night. She felt as dishonored as if she'd actually committed the sin he accused her of.

In the morning her eyes were red and puffy, and no amount of cold water would have erased the evidence of the torturous night. At the breakfast table there was strained silence, then a lot of nervous small talk about the freshness of the eggs and the saltiness of the ham. Felicia stared into space, unhearing, and Grant glared across at her.

Undaunted, Ilse went on planning her day. As she left the table, she stopped to stand behind Grant's chair. She'd braided her hair into long plaits and wound them like a regal coronet around the top of her head. She was wearing a pink peasant blouse that made her look as apple-cheeked as a serving girl in a Bavarian beer hall.

"You must go with me into Clarita Valley this morning, Grant. I have errands to do and then we will have lunch at the tavern I saw there. Felicia wants us to take time out for fun," she said, giving everyone the first big smile since her arrival. Apparently the rupture between Grant and Felicia was obvious to her and brightened her up tremendously.

Grant had finished eating and was lighting a cigarette. "All right. I think we've earned some good times," he said, blowing a stream of smoke toward Felicia.

Ilse bent down to take the cigarette from his lips. "Naughty boy. You promised me you were going to stop this filthy habit." She impudently ground out the cigarette on his plate.

Rather than resenting her for taking such liberties, Grant reached up behind him and took her hand in his. "You know I only smoke when the stress gets to me. But I think you have a better idea. Let's go out and do something different."

For the next few days Ilse and Grant were coming and going in the car constantly, often failing to show up for meals, and when they did join the others, regaling them with stories of their escapades in all the local bars and cafés. One night they arrived back at the lodge so late that Felicia was already in bed, and she could hear them whispering and giggling as they fixed a nightcap and put on a disco record to dance.

The next day Felicia sat for hours at the sewing machine in her room with a bolt of flowered chintz, making curtains for the guest rooms, working diligently but unable to block out thoughts of what was going on around her. It was obvious to her that Grant appreciated Ilse's company. He no doubt saw her as a woman with no child, no lodge to rehabilitate, no responsibilities to limit her, and ready at any moment to lead him down rollicking paths of amusement toward the forgetfulness he needed.

Her mind and the sewing machine were both whirring along so fast she didn't hear Nadine come into the room.

"Hey, Cinderella. Your stepsisters have gone off to the ball. What are you going to do about it?"

Felicia rubbed at her tired eyes and leaned back to laugh at Nadine. "What do you mean?"

"Ilse has taken that ex-husband of yours off with her again. They took skis with them so they'll probably be gone all day again."

"He likes to have a good time," Felicia said.

"He's not having a good time. He's trying to look like he's having a good time. Is he trying to make you jealous?"

"I don't know." Felicia knew she couldn't keep anything from her close friend. "I can't help but wonder about their relationship. You know, I found out he's known her a long time, even before we split up."

"She's the one who told you that, I'm sure. She's working her head off to make it look like they're more than just good friends."

"And you don't believe it?"

Nadine stood up and swaggered around the room as if she were talking about herself. "I think you could get him back with one little twitch of those trim hips of yours." She turned to peer at Felicia over

175

her shoulder. "And a wink from one of those big blue eyes."

Felicia almost laughed at Nadine's antics, but her grief was too great. "I thought so a few days ago, but now it's too late."

"What happened? I noticed the wind-chill factor take a drop around here. Did he find out about Sally?"

"Worse than that. He thinks that I was carrying on with some imaginary fellow while still married to him. He thinks I ran off to marry Sally's father."

"Oh, no." Nadine recognized the real tragedy of Grant's mistake. "Now he's going all out to get back at you with these wild times with Ilse. So, you don't think you'll ever get him back?"

"Nadine, there's no point in trying to recapture anything that there once was between us. I knew five years ago he wouldn't want to be a father to his child, and he hasn't changed a bit. He still prefers the life of a jet setter."

"How can you resist giving it a try? I mean, he's just about the most gorgeous man I've ever laid eyes on, Felicia. If Dan Fowler had looked like that . . ."

Both girls began to smile, grateful that they'd left behind those awful days at the ski shop.

"If Dan Fowler could see you the way you look now, Nadine — I think you've dropped off a dozen pounds with all your hard work around here — he'd drag you back into the stockroom with your ledger book still in your hand."

"Thanks for calling me a vamp, Felicia. But I can't say the mountain air has done much for you. You've turned into a sweat-shop drudge. Now get out of here and take a break, will you?"

"All right, all right. Stop nagging," Felicia said, realizing the suggestion was a good one. Her arms and shoulders felt stiff and tired. "I'll put on those cross-country skis and take a little tour of my meadow, how's that?"

Felicia had not done much cross-country skiing, and the light, low-cut boots felt strange to her as she put them on. It was even more difficult to get used to the ski binding which left her heel free to lift up from the skis as she moved forward, sliding across the snow in long strides, her arms poling her forward in opposite motion to her feet.

The day was cold, with an overcast of clouds that paled the sun. But the snow was ideal, granular with large ice crystals, so she made good progress, moving quickly across the meadow and along the base of the mountain.

The day passed quickly, and she knew she'd been right to take on this taxing physical activity. She'd always found it impossible to mull over her troubles when she was involved in strenuous exercise. But the sky overhead was darkening under a blanket of storm clouds, and she began to think about heading for home. She had come farther from the lodge than she'd planned, and if it began to snow, she would make slower progress.

She saw a place where she could make a shortcut down a steep knoll and rejoin her path at the bottom. As she aimed her skis downhill, she caught one of the edges on a rock, and she had to check her speed. But her effort came too late and she tumbled into a fall, rolling over and over, landing at the bottom of the hill in a twisted heap, one leg bent beneath her.

She sat for a moment, cursing herself for such clumsiness. As she started to straighten her legs in front of her, she felt the warning of a cramp near the top of her right boot, and she reached down to touch that ankle. The stab of pain she felt then gave her an equal feeling of fear. If she'd hurt her ankle, her return to the lodge might be long and painful.

She pushed herself upright onto her good leg, and then tried to take one hesitant step forward. A fiery flame shot up her leg, burning the breath out of her lungs, and forcing her to fall back into the snow. The pain was shooting at her upward from the damaged ankle, and she began to realize just how badly she'd been hurt in what had seemed such an innocent fall, so much like countless other falls she'd taken.

She knew she could not put any weight on her right foot, so when she got up to make another try, she used one ski pole as a crutch, sliding forward a few inches at a time until she was exhausted. She saw a clump of fir trees just ahead, and she crawled through the snow until she reached the comfort of that small shelter, and huddled against some fallen branches, defeated.

The full enormity of her situation then brought her to near panic. Unable to move, she could freeze to death here in the snow. It would be hours before Nadine became alarmed, and even then she wasn't capable of coming on a search. And Grant was off somewhere having fun with Ilse.

She tried to remember her winter survival skills. Taking off the long knitted muffler that she'd worn wrapped around her neck, she tied it over her head, so that her body heat would not escape. She knew that she had to stay awake, and keep herself moving as much as possible, but when she made an attempt to stand up later, she found the pain so overwhelming that she almost fainted, and she resigned herself to a long cold wait, but a wait for what, she didn't know.

She roused herself to wave her arms about in the air from time to time, but they grew more numb and unfeeling each time. She wondered how much time had passed. The sky was dark, for the threatening storm clouds had caused evening to come early. She sang old fireside songs into the darkness, and recited the only poem she knew, *The Owl and the Pussycat*, several times in an effort to keep her spirits up, but then the quiet of the night closed in on her, shutting down all her attempts at optimism.

Being so alone, and so helpless, not knowing if anyone would come to find her in time, she had to struggle against the haunting nightmares of childhood, the horrible visions of disaster that teased her, taunting at her as the long hours passed and she shook with uncontrollable chills.

If only she could let go and sleep! Maybe if she curled up into a tight warm ball, resting her head on the soft pine needles and closing her eyes, she could think of happier times and warmer places — and not be afraid.

She heard her brother calling to her to come inside to dinner. She heard Grant calling to her to ski down the race course just once more. She heard Andy and Jeff calling her to come see the kitchen now that it was painted. Then she sat bolt upright and realized she'd been asleep.

I can't do that. I have to stay awake. I'll try clapping my hands, patting my face.

But she fell back against her bower of branches, depressed and weary, letting the frightening refuge of sleep overpower her again. The throbbing in her cold legs and arms invaded even her dreams, and her extremities twitched painfully while her breathing slowed as time passed and she sank deeper into unconsciousness.

"Felicia! Where are you? Felicia!"

There was that damned dream again.

"Felicia, I'm coming. Where are you?"

How nice to dream that Grant was coming for her. How comforting to hear his voice and imagine that he was looking for her, that he wanted to find her. She closed her eyes, willing the dream to continue.

"Felicia?" It seemed so close now.

"Grant. Is that really you? Grant. Here I am!"

All at once she realized that it wasn't a dream. Someone was looking for her. She could hear the crunch of snow and the thrashing aside of heavy branches. Now someone was slipping and sliding down the very hill where she'd tumbled.

"Oh, Grant. Please come quick. Please find me!" She thought she was screaming but realized her voice was pitifully small and then knew just how weak she was.

"My God, Felicia, what happened to you?" Grant was standing over her, breathing so hard that she could see great clouds of steam coming from his mouth in fast gulps. She struggled to get up, thrashing about with exultant relief as he helped her.

"I twisted my ankle, and then I couldn't step on it, and I couldn't get home."

She threw herself against him, crying and babbling senselessly, letting loose all the fear that she'd tried to keep bottled up inside her. She didn't care what he thought of her now; she was too overcome with gratitude that he was here.

"Oh, Grant, I thought I was going to die.

I didn't think anyone would ever come looking for me, and I would freeze to death here. It was so cold, and so dark, and I was so frightened."

"Shh, Felicia. You're all right now." He smoothed her hair out of her face and back under the muffler. "Here, let loose of me a minute. I've got a flask in my pocket for you. Drink something quickly."

She felt the metal container tremble slightly in his hands as he held it against her lips and realized that he'd had a long walk through the cold night.

"Oh, it burns. What is it?"

"I had Nadine warm up some rum before I set out after you. Here, take off your gloves and hold the flask, it will feel good to your cold hands."

She did as she was told, still savoring the hot flow of liquor which had revived her with a reeling urge for self-preservation. She began stamping her good leg and shaking her head.

"That's right, move about all that you can. Now let's see that foot."

"Don't touch it. It hurts," she cried as he stooped down and gripped her ankle.

"Well, you can't walk on it, that's for sure."

He picked her up in his arms as if she

weighed nothing and began heading for home through the snow. While she had been sleeping and dreaming, it had started to snow, and now she could see the light dusting of flakes on his hair, but she wasn't afraid that the snow that was falling would increase, that a full-scale southern Sierras blizzard had begun. Neither did she worry that Grant would not have the strength to carry her all the way back. And she had no fear that he would lose his way, even with the fresh snow already beginning to fill in his tracks. All of her fears were over, and she had only to bounce along in the safety of his arms.

"You were quite right to be afraid," Grant said, expelling the words in bunches with his heavy breaths as he trudged with some difficulty through the snow. "The temperature's fallen to ten degrees. You never would have made it through the night."

The freezing night air was nipping at her face, burning the skin on the two thin paths where tears still dampened her cheeks. She buried her face in the curly lambskin collar at Grant's neck, taking comfort from the close sounds of his heavy breathing.

"Thank you, Grant, for coming after

me," she whispered, not trying to make him hear her, saying it more as a prayer.

"When Ilse and I came back from skiing to change for dinner, Nadine was worried sick." He seemed very anxious to give away all the credit for the rescue.

It seemed a minor miracle to Felicia that Grant could get her home so quickly, never stopping to rest. Like a huge Abominable Snowman, he kept his steady pace through the night, as the snow piled up a flaky hood of white on his hair and eyebrows.

Soon they saw the lodge just across the meadow, with the welcome of every window ablaze with light. When they came inside in a cloud of snow, everyone came hovering around, full of questions. But Grant dropped Felicia onto a chair and began barking out orders.

"Sally, you can stop kissing your mother. She's fine. But she needs a hot bath, and quickly. Can you go up and fill her tub?"

Sally hurried off on her mission. Now, letting his concern show more obviously, he told Nadine, "Her body temperature has to be brought up as quickly as possible. You boil some water, and bring it upstairs right away. With the bottle of rum, some brown sugar and spices, and a pat of butter."

"Hot buttered rum? That's rather fancy

treatment for a girl who foolishly gets lost in the snow, isn't it?" Ilse interjected.

"Ilse, do you think you know how to put a child to bed?" Grant asked to stop her interference. "You take care of Sally. Make sure she's not worried about her mother."

Ilse went upstairs with a sulky look on her face as Grant picked Felicia up again and carried her to her room.

"Good night, Mommy. I'm glad you're home and safe," Sally said, leaving the room with Ilse. "Your bathtub is all ready for you."

When they had left, Grant carried Felicia into the bathroom and plopped her down on the floor.

"Now strip off those clothes and get into the hot water."

She stared at him a moment, wondering if he planned to stay and watch, but he turned around and left the room, and she did as she had been told.

The hot bath felt wonderful, and she could feel her body respond as it thawed her slowly, bringing a tingling along her length, and subduing, somewhat, the throbbing in her ankle. A steamy layer of vapor hovered over the top of the water, and she breathed it deeply inside of herself, as if it were capable of reaching the vital interior regions of her body where she was still cold. She closed her eyes and leaned her head back against the porcelain rim of the tub, at last letting herself relax and drift into the half sleep that had been such an ominous symptom when she'd been on the dark hillside.

"All right, bath time is over," Grant said as he opened the door and walked right in. She sat up so suddenly that water sloshed up the sides of the tub, perilously close to brimming over onto the tile floor. Her hands flew up to cover her bare chest, and she looked at him with wide-eyed surprise.

"Don't act so modest with me. I've admired your naked body often enough. I don't plan to embarrass you by leering."

She noticed that he was carrying her granny nightgown over one arm as if he fully intended to dress her himself.

"Get me a towel, would you?" she asked, noticing that although his eyes moved familiarly over her nude body, he registered no reaction. She could see no suggestive cocked eyebrow, or amorous wetting of the lips with his tongue as he had playfully done in the past as he studied her curves. She felt an odd disappointment, as if her failure to arouse him anymore was a sure sign that their passion was dead, as cold and without function as a dirty glacier making its way slowly to the end, to the sea.

When she seemed to be moving too slowly to satisfy him, he reached down to pull her by one hand, and steadied her with that hand as she stepped onto the bath mat. As she dried herself, he stood watching, impersonally and without patience, finally taking the towel from her and patting it up her back, which she'd turned toward him. He reached around her waist, and stroked the towel up her body toward her breasts, then let the towel drop to the floor to check his work with flat, hard pats of his hand.

"I think you've warmed up enough," he said with no seduction in his tone. As he cupped her breasts in his two hands, Felicia felt herself sway against him, suddenly enervated by the rapid changes in temperature that were rocketing through her body.

But he didn't seem to notice, and his next words were spoken clinically, with the detachment of a medical expert, as his interest shifted to other parts of her body.

"Let me feel those fingers; they're okay, no sign of frostbite. Here, slip this over your head while I check your ankle."

She slid into the nightgown and watched

him crouch beside her to probe and press the skin along her ankle to assess the damage.

"There's very little swelling. I don't think it's broken. You can wrap it tomorrow if necessary."

He stood up and looked at her, and she felt the oppression of the humid, heavy air in the room, still swirling in steamy clouds. He reached toward her, and she felt her body tremble in anticipation of what he might do. But he only reached into her hair to pull the pins from it that she'd used to hold her hair up out of the water.

As he pulled her hair into place about her face, he said shortly, "Your bangs need trimming."

"I know that. I've been busy," she said, limping to follow him as he headed into the bedroom.

Her bed had been turned back, the pillows piled ready for her, and on a tray on the bedside table Nadine had left the makings of her drink. While she settled herself beneath the quilt, he went to work mixing her a hot buttered rum. Felicia noticed with a smile that Nadine had left two mugs, but Grant wasn't fixing one for himself.

He handed her the drink and watched her sip it, sitting down on the edge of the bed beside her just as he'd done a few nights before. She felt the urge to snuggle down into position for one of his fabulous massages, but he was watching her intently to make sure she swallowed every mouthful of the hot liquid.

The butter that floated on top was melting, and the rum below it almost sizzling with heat, but she drank the hot buttered rum as thirstily as if she were completely dehydrated. As she sipped, she watched him bend toward her into the beam of the bedside lamp.

She noticed how haggard he looked and realized the adventure of the night had taken its toll on him. He'd gone out alone into a snowstorm looking for her, not knowing if he could find her, following her tracks and calling her name into the darkness. Then he'd carried her back for miles, never slowing his pace, in a hurry to get her to warmth and bring her back to life again.

She reached up and placed her free hand along the side of his face, wishing there was some way she could soothe away the deep crevices near his eyes, the tired downturn of his thin lips. The skin of his face felt like leather, the soft calf of an expensive book binding, and she felt as she touched it that this volume had been closed to her, that she would never get to hear the end of the melancholy story it contained.

"Thank you," she said. "Thanks for coming to get me."

"You're welcome," he said with formality. "I think I got there just in time." And the snowball-cold look of his eyes told her that he would have done the same for any human being in peril.

"And thank you for not giving me a lecture on ski safety," she smiled. "I know I shouldn't have gone cross-country skiing alone. And I know I should have carried a knapsack of survival supplies."

"I'm trying to forget that I was your coach. You're a big girl now; you don't need my constant critique." He turned to the tray to fix her another drink, but she was already feeling the overstimulation of the one she'd drunk too quickly, so she shook her head.

"I suppose you're going to be leaving soon," she said tentatively.

"I'll stay with you a few more minutes. I want to see the color come back to your face." He turned away from her. "I'm not going to force myself into bed with you like last time, if that's what you're afraid of."

The last time he'd been here with her, he had warmed her, melted away the years of loneliness and longing, and stimulated back into awareness all the ice-hard, frozen, lost feelings she thought would never return. Now tonight he'd done the same thing, stirred her to life again, but with only skin-deep physical gestures. Her heart still cried out for his deeper healing, but now that he believed she had betrayed him, she knew he would never again open himself to her.

"I meant, you'll be leaving Deer Meadow. You said you could only stay a short while."

"Well, I've finally gotten a lead on that financing, so as soon as that's settled, I'll be on my way. It's not easy to be here, to be around you, you know," he said, folding his arms across his chest with a movement as abrupt as the slam of a door.

"Grant, it's not easy for me, either. When you said those awful things about me the other night, it hurt me to think you could believe them." She blinked rapidly to keep her eyes clear so that she could watch his reaction. If only he would take her into his arms and tell her he'd been wrong to believe her capable of cheating on him.

"You can't hide the truth, this time. It's right there in black and white, handed to me by a school official. An accurate document of the activities of a faithless wife." His posture was as stiff and unyielding as a ski carnival figure carved of snow.

"If you'd just listen to my story," she pleaded.

His hands shot out to take her roughly by the shoulders. He pulled her forward and back against the pillows in punctuation of his words.

"I don't want to hear any more of your lies!"

"All right, Grant, no more lies." The rum that was pulsing through her veins with its hot stream of false courage was almost pushing the words from her mouth. But he had stopped shaking her, and dropped his head forward to rest it on one of his hands at her shoulders, almost burying his face into the flannel that bunched up beneath his grasping fingers.

"If only you didn't have such a maddening effect on me," he mumbled. "If only I could keep my reason intact and not fall for all your fables and myths."

Just then a sharp knock at the door interrupted him, and he sat back as if he'd found himself in a compromising position, a place where he did not want to be.

He cleared his throat deliberately and with great difficulty, then called out, "Who is it?"

Ilse took that as an invitation to burst open the door and come in. Seeing them so close together on the bed, Felicia's cheeks now fully aflame with color, and Grant's face an exhausted mask of hidden emotion, her nostrils flared quickly with surprise, and she drew herself up to her full imposing height.

"Now that the household has returned to normal, there are some duties you should see to, Grant."

"What is it, Ilse?"

"Some important mail has come today, and you must look it over. There's a letter from that businessman in San Francisco you've been trying to reach."

"Yes, I'd better see to that."

He stood up and turned to explain to Felicia. "This may be what we're waiting for. If this is the man with the money, then we can get this project going."

He followed Ilse out, and Felicia was left to think. Grant was anxious to get her business affairs in order. He'd been in one place too long. And any place where she was probably seemed especially confining to him. It was time for him to be let loose, to fly and be free again. Any day now he would be gone, and the heartbreaking re-union would be over.

CHAPTER EIGHT

The next day was Saturday, and with Sally home from school Felicia wanted to spend time with her, tending to her needs and making her feel confident that her mother was all right, unaffected by the fearsome experience of being lost in the snow.

"Come on, love, now that your hair is washed, hop up here on this chair." She wrapped Sally's shoulders in a towel and faced her toward the mirror over her dresser just as if she were a fine lady in a beauty salon.

"We've let this go too long," she said, combing the hair down into Sally's eyes, and then snipping away at it, so that little brown bits fell all over the towel and the floor.

Felicia stood back to study her child's reflection. She tried not to see Grant's eyes looking back at her. She concentrated instead on the uneven slice of hair that now dipped across the child's forehead.

"A little more here, a little more here." Her scissors gave brisk clicking sounds as she worked, and she hobbled from one side to the other, favoring her strong leg.

"Is your foot going to be okay, Mommy?"

"Oh, yes. I've wrapped my ankle in an elastic bandage, but that's just for today. By tomorrow I'm sure I'll be fine."

"Excuse me for interrupting your morning rituals, ladies." Grant was standing in the doorway of her room, leaning his imposing length against one doorjamb as if he'd been there watching them for some time.

"Hi, coach. We're having our haircuts," Sally said pertly.

"I can see that," he said, observing the turban of towel around Felicia's head that meant she was next in line to undergo the scissors.

"Almost through, baby. Hold still and quit twisting around in the chair," Felicia said.

Grant made no move to leave but instead watched the process with mild interest, and Felicia began to suspect he was waiting to talk to her alone.

"All done. Why don't you go down and dry your hair in front of the fire?" Felicia kissed Sally's cheek, then pulled the cape away from her shoulders and helped her down.

"Okay, Mommy. Are you going to do yours now? Just the same way?"

"Exactly," she laughed. "The same as always."

The child skipped from the room, stopping to give Grant a playful swipe on his pants leg, and then rushed off down the hall, pretending she was in danger of being pursued.

Felicia sat down in front of the mirror and began working on her own hair, just as if Grant were not there.

"I'm just doing as told, coach. You said my hair needed a trim."

"If you want to see anything of the world, it sure does," he said, and this morning he seemed rested and again capable of reacting to her politely, giving her a restrained smile that camouflaged his hostility.

"Did you have some business matter to discuss with me?" she said, glancing at him in the mirror. She had no desire to resurrect their personal problems this morning.

"It's about Leslie Talbot, the man who wrote me from San Francisco."

"The money man?"

"Yes, he wants to come and look us over."

"Oh, no. When?"

"He says he'll be arriving tomorrow night."

197

"I guess we'd better roll out that red carpet again," she said with a resigned sigh, devoid of enthusiasm.

"There's another problem . . ."

Grant seemed unsure of how to go on. She put down the scissors to swivel sideways on her chair and face him directly. "Yes? What is it?"

"When I first wrote to him about investing in a ski resort, I told him my wife owned the property, and that I didn't want to finance it myself because I felt an outside investor would be more impartial, could make more logical decisions, and . . ."

"And . . ."

"Well, I guess he misunderstood. He thinks we're still married."

"You'll have to set him straight on that."

"After reading his letter, I'm not so sure I want to."

"What do you mean?"

"He thinks we need money because we're a struggling young couple, trying to start up a family business. It seems he and his wife once started up a clothing business together, that's how they made their fortune. He's rather sentimental about it."

"And you think that when he hears about our sordid divorce, he'll run off as if we are tainted somehow?"

"Yes, I do. He's a very conservative man, and a big believer in social stability — rock-solid families and all that."

She turned back to the mirror and pressed one hand down on her damp bangs while with the other she ran the scissors in a straight cutting motion in line with her eyebrows. She was making a great effort to appear calm, in spite of all the unsettling news he was laying at her feet with so little emotional involvement of his own. He went on, his dark eyes seeming to smolder like a dead fire, with only obscuring smoke and a noticeable absence of flame.

"Frankly, I don't know where I can find another such likely prospect as Mr. Talbot. He's interested in skiing, and he has money to invest. Felicia, you need the money before summer comes, and you need a lot of it if you're going to be ready to open for guests next winter. Think about it."

"You're suggesting we put on a bit of a show? That we hide the truth, just for his benefit?"

"I wouldn't usually suggest such a lie . . ." he began.

"But since I'm so practiced at lying, you figure why not try it, is that it?"

He ignored her barb. "It will only be for a day or two."

"I suppose it's a very small deception. After all, we were man and wife when we bought this property and made our plans for it." She sat leaning one elbow on the dresser, resting her head on her clenched fist. "I wouldn't agree to this if anyone would be hurt by it. In spite of what you think, I've never told a falsehood except to save someone's feelings."

"What a noble excuse," he muttered, then swallowed his words quickly as if he'd promised himself he would keep his reactions to her in check. "Then you agree?" he asked, expressionless.

"I agree if we can think of a way to keep Sally completely out of it. I won't have her trained in deceit."

"Since he's arriving after she's in bed Sunday, and she goes off to school Monday, I doubt if she'll see much of our guest, and we'll enlist Nadine and Ilse's help to keep her occupied elsewhere."

"Oh, that's right," she said. "We have to get them in on this."

She was already beginning to wonder if this was such a good idea. A fabricated story, acted out for whatever good reason, had ways of growing into a monster in time. It began lurking about, refusing to leave you alone, introducing itself to all your friends, and feeding off of every little added lie that was necessary to keep it alive, until it had grown so suffocatingly huge you couldn't break free of it. She knew that monster better than most people. It had lived with her and controlled her life too long. But maybe after just a few more days Mr. Talbot would be gone and Grant would leave here for good and she could begin her new life without the constant fear of exposure. Perhaps she would soon have that monster caged.

Grant went off to present the plan to Nadine and Ilse, and the rest of the weekend was spent in hectic preparations for the important new guest. Ilse watched Grant move his things into one of the upstairs rooms with a moody new lack of comment. Nadine was more helpful, working with Felicia to scrub and clean a guest room until it glistened.

By Sunday evening the lodge was spruced up in readiness for the curtain to rise, and that quiet descended over it that meant the performance was ready to begin. The fire was stoked high, Sally was asleep, and Nadine and Ilse had retired to their rooms. The place was filled with the scent of tangy spices simmering in the kitchen, and Felicia was nervously knitting by the fire.

"Everything looks perfect," Grant said, coming to join her. "Including you." He gave her wardrobe choices an assessing scan. She was wearing a lacy mohair sweater of pale blue over a floor-length tweed hostess skirt.

"Why, thank you," she said, guarding her expression while she tried to figure out why he'd forced himself to give her a compliment.

"While our guest is here, we're going to have to put our personal dissension aside," he said.

"That's just as well. We've argued over it quite enough."

"But it won't be easy to forget."

"Then just pretend it's forgotten," she advised. And just at that moment, when she was afraid the waiting would dissolve her tenuous commitment to the plan, she heard the sound of a car, and Grant motioned to her to come and join him at the front door. A small gray-haired woman, all bundled in fur, came through the door first, followed by her slightly taller husband.

"Mrs. Talbot, Mr. Talbot, I'm Grant Mitchell. Welcome to our lodge."

Mr. Talbot stepped around his wife to shake Grant's hand.

"Glad to meet you, young man. I've

heard great things about you and those resorts you've planned in Europe. I've always wanted to be involved in such a project from the start."

"Well, Deer Meadow is at its start, no doubt about that. And we hope you'll decide to become involved in it. Meet my wife."

Grant put his arm around her with a studied pose of affection.

"Mrs. Mitchell, glad to meet you. This is my wife, Eleanor Talbot."

"Oh, please," Felicia insisted with a special emphasis, "call me Felicia." She couldn't bear to hear herself called Mrs. Mitchell ever again.

"And call me Eleanor," the shy woman said from behind her husband, shrugging herself out of her fur without any help.

"You must be cold after your long drive. Come and sit by the fire and have a glass of mulled wine with us," Felicia offered, and the couple accepted gladly, taking a curious peek around the candlelit room as they went to sit down.

Felicia walked beside Grant, and he spontaneously gave her an affectionate hug, accompanying it with a sly wink as he showed off how easy it was for him to cover up his true feelings. Flustered, Felicia went to fetch the ingredients from the kitchen, and then Grant began an elaborate show of mixing the Burgundy wine with the hot mixture of spices and citrus juices she had heated.

"In Switzerland they heat the *glühwein* by thrusting a hot poker into the glass just before serving it," he said, looking as domesticated as the most dutiful husband as he served everyone. "But you'll have to settle for my more subtle style."

"If you're hungry, we'll have some fondue a little later," Felicia offered, trying not to appear overeager to please them and already reproaching herself for this pretense they were putting up for people she could tell she was going to like. She turned to Mrs. Talbot.

"I understand you work with your husband in the clothing business, is that right?"

Her husband answered for her. "Yes, we're Swim Right bathing suits. That is, we founded the company that makes the suits. And we're adding a line of ski clothes next season. Maybe we can make a nice tie-in with your lodge here. It surely seems a promising place."

Grant began describing his ideas for how the mountain behind them could be cleared and groomed for ski slopes, and he wove fascinating tales of his plans for the lodge facilities. Felicia watched him as he paced before the fire, gesturing with his broad hands as he made them all picture what it could be like. She was surprised to hear him describe for the first time his imaginative blueprint for the future, worked out in great detail, and she began to have new respect for the visionary nature of his talents. No wonder he was sought by the master planners of ski resorts all over the world, she thought, and Mr. Talbot seemed similarly impressed.

"You certainly remind me of myself at your age," he told Grant, patting proudly at the round belly he'd grown since then. "Those are very fancy dreams."

Felicia stepped closer to Grant. "And I think he can make them come true," she said, realizing as she spoke that she was using words of loving pride. She was waving the banner of her love in front of two near strangers, when she had spent five years convincing herself that it did not exist.

"That's what I like to see, confidence!" Mr. Talbot said exuberantly. "How about some more of that wine, Grant?" He held his glass out. "You're a lucky man. You have a beautiful and loyal wife."

Grant stopped the ladle in midair, and turned his penetrating glance upon Felicia. "She's just as beautiful as the day I first met her," he said.

Felicia noticed his pointed attempt to ignore Mr. Talbot's description of her as "loyal." Grant could not agree that on this score she was beyond reproach. He was certain she had been a promiscuous and unfaithful wife, and she knew that this charade of husband and wife that they were acting out must be uncomfortable for him. He was only going through with it because he wanted her financially settled and permanently off his mind.

"How about that fondue you promised?" Grant asked. She had been distracted, unconsciously stroking the smooth skin between her neck and collarbone while her thoughts wandered far away. Now she noticed that Grant was watching the path of her fingers with unblinking concentration. He leaned over to squeeze her arm tenderly, apparently willing to go to any length to convince his audience of his devotion.

She brought the fondue pot to the coffee table and began melting the cheese and tearing the French bread into small pieces. When the cheese was bubbling its fragrance through the room, she passed out long fondue forks and they all began to eat.

"It's an old custom," Grant explained, "if the bread falls off a woman's fork into the fondue, she must kiss her partner."

"And what if the man's bread is lost?" Talbot asked, waving an empty fork in the air.

"Then he must refill everyone's glass."

And so they passed the rest of the evening in cheery company with these new friends, with glasses being frequently refilled as the Swiss cheese was consumed. Grant seemed to take sadistic delight in doing battle with Felicia's fondue fork, inspiring the laughter of the Talbots. But each time she lost the battle and he leaned across the coffee table to plant a passionless kiss on her lips, it was as if another log had been thrown onto the fire. She could feel the hot wine moving through her, warming her to wait breathlessly for the next prized kiss he would claim. She began to fear she would throw herself too recklessly into this act.

Grant appeared to be imperturbable in this unaccustomed role, but she became so jumpy that once when her hand brushed accidentally across his thigh as she reached toward the low table, she pulled it back so hastily she bumped her wineglass and set it rocking, giving the Talbots an apologetic smile. Grant calmly closed his hand over hers and held it to still the trembling.

After stifling a yawn or two, Mr. and Mrs. Talbot finally admitted they would have to turn in and call short the good times.

"I'll show them to their rooms, sweetness," Grant said to Felicia. "You go on upstairs. I'll be along in a moment."

"Breakfast is whenever you get to the kitchen and introduce yourself to my friend and cook, Nadine," she said, for some reason a bit nervously unsettled.

"Good night, Felicia dear," Mrs. Talbot said. "And thank you for making us feel so welcome on short notice."

Felicia headed toward the stairs, her shoulders sagging somewhat with the relief of having endured the drama they'd acted out this evening. A looming shadow on the wall overtook her, and she realized that Grant was following her.

"I can't let my darling wife go off to bed without a good night kiss," he said with a wide teasing smile that showed how he enjoyed using this advantage to annoy her.

He reached one arm out to her and placed his hand at the back of her neck, his long fingers reaching into her blond hair as he pulled her face toward him. She involuntarily closed her eyes as her focus dimmed with expectation. He touched her mouth with his, lightly at first, then with deepening intensity, never releasing his masterful hold on her until he felt her slight stirring of response. His fingertips moved with enticing delicacy at the back of her neck, pressing just enough to alarm every nerve along the sensitive curve beneath her hair, and causing her to quiver in answer to his touch. His practiced lips knew just how to arouse her, and she envisioned fanciful dreams of a husband's promise of a good night yet to come. The room seemed to be spinning around her as she fought to regain her hold on reality before she was lost completely in this performance of his.

As soon as she drew her lips away, he said with a husky drawl, "Wait for me." She wasn't sure it was said for the benefit of the others in the room. Her face turned hot and flushed as she hurried upstairs to her room.

He must have ushered the Talbots to their quarters like any eager husband with a young wife waiting upstairs, for within a few moments he opened the door and came into her room. She had, indeed, waited for him, standing by the window, studying their mountain.

He came to stand behind her, and he put his arms around her waist and looked out, too, at the view.

"I think we carried things off rather well, don't you?" he asked.

"I know they liked the place," she said, tipping her head to the side with drowsy satisfaction to rest it against his chin, completely comfortable with the old habit.

"I think they approved of my plans."

"I did too. My own ideas were not so ambitious. You've made me see what a wonderful place this could be." He'd also made her see how it could be to act the hostess here with a host she loved, to share the years of growth that were ahead with him, with her husband.

"I knew you could convince them you were a happy wife. After all, you had me convinced, even when you were desperate to get away from me."

She twisted away from him and turned to stare. "Did you have to bring that up again?"

"Forgive me. I can see you'd rather we keep the congenial act going, pretend nothing ever happened to spoil things. Pretend that *he* never came between us."

"You were the one who said we must forget all that for the time being," she said, her complacent mood shattered. He had lulled her just enough to make this thrusting new offensive more injuring.

"I've tried, but I can't stop picturing that man who destroyed our marriage. He'll always loom up between us."

She fervently wished now that she'd never invented the man who was supposed to be Sally's father. How much simpler it would have been if she'd been mature enough then to face him with the truth: that she wanted to have their baby, and that she would not let him follow her or try to interfere with her decision.

"Forget that other man, will you?" she said, at last ready to face the consequences of a full revelation. "I never did remarry. There wasn't any second husband." At last the final deception was removed.

Grant's face was inscrutable for just a moment while he absorbed the meaning of her words; then he shook his head sadly.

"You mean that bum never even married you? All that was lies too? You went through all of it alone, you had no husband with you for the birth, he didn't even give his child a legal father? And still you moon around over the man who abandoned you, making excuses for him."

"I've never tried to defend what happened. You've never given me a chance. Now let me tell you how ridiculous it is for you to hate that man so much, so we can both forget him forever." But before she could go on with her explanation, he raised his hand to stop her, and she flinched as if a real blow had been struck.

"I'll give you a chance right now to show me how hard you're trying to forget him." His eyes were flaring with an angry passion as he grabbed her around the waist and began pushing her backward toward the bed. "Let's see if you can make love to me this time and mean it. Let's see if you're really willing to pretend he never existed!"

"What are you doing?" she demanded as she felt her legs pressed against the bed, ready to crumble beneath her.

"I'm going to finish this little drama. Act three, coming up."

She tried to twist from his grasp, but her struggles only seemed to heighten the eroticism of the situation. As she writhed miserably in his arms, she felt his body harden against hers, and she felt the stimulating effects as her breasts brushed briskly against his rocklike chest. She felt as if they were performing some ritualistic dance together.

"Go ahead, lure me again with those traitorous kisses. Make me believe it's me you want," he breathed hoarsely near her ear.

He seemed to be purposely baiting her, testing that infamous temper of hers. She suspected that he was pushing her as far as he could with this cruel trick, trying to force her to throw him out so that he'd be purged of his physical desire for her once and for all.

Inside she was seething, but she didn't want to let him know how much she cared, how much it mattered to her that he was treating her with such contempt.

"Are you trying to punish me?" she charged. "Must I do penance for my sins?" She had begun to believe he was seriously planning to take her in anger, make her suffer degradation at his hands in payment for her illicit affair. "Well, I have nothing to be ashamed of. I will not let you cheapen me like this."

She let some of the angry steam that was binding up escape through her safety valve, thrusting out her lower lip to blow the clean light hair over her forehead so that it exploded into a blond sunburst before it resettled onto her face.

Grant watched her and she could tell he had correctly measured the characteristic mannerism by the way he dropped his clutching hands from where they were riding roughshod over her body. The moment of reckoning had passed.

"I don't want you to touch me ever again!" she stammered. "You are not to kiss me or come near my room again, do you hear me? I don't care what the Talbots think. I want no more of your abuse."

"Sorry, sweetness," he said, making the word seem an epithet. "I thought I'd detected some vital signs still functioning in that cold body of yours when I kissed you downstairs." He turned to walk toward the door, leaving her breathless, her face shiny from beads of perspiration, after the unconsummated battle of wills. She hadn't yet been able to cut through his accusations with the truth. There was no reasoning with his blind prejudices against her.

His last words were cold and meant to hurt. "I hope you enjoy your lonely bed. You might just consider this. Sometimes second choice is better than no man at all to warm your feet against."

As she fell asleep that night, she answered him in a subdued whisper from beneath the comforter. *You're my first and only choice, Grant, and you always have been.* And she considered with an overwhelming sense of hopelessness this love for him which could never be expressed.

The next day she sat dejectedly having an early morning cup of coffee in the lounge with the Talbots when Ilse came to join them. Felicia expected her to launch into a long speech on resort management, but she was curiously taciturn, cradling a cup in tightly coiled fingers, scarcely drinking from it as she huddled on a corner of one couch and glowered at everyone. She sat up straighter when Grant appeared on the landing at the top of the stairs.

"Good morning, everyone. Sorry I slept a bit late." He stretched his long arms above him, sensuously extending his sinewy arm muscles. "I hope Felicia explained to you that I needed some extra sleep," he said, his eyes squinting at them suggestively. Then he yawned as if he were a sublimely contented man.

Ilse expelled a disgusted sigh in Felicia's direction, then got up to go into the kitchen, her knee-high black boots giving stomping sounds that Felicia hoped the Talbots wouldn't notice.

"I thought I'd take Leslie and Eleanor on a short hike up the mountain today for some skiing," Grant said, coming down the stairs and taking up a position beside Felicia, reaching out toward her but then carefully making sure his flesh did not come into contact with hers. "I suppose you'd rather stay here and tend to your chores," he said, giving her the excuse she needed to be excluded from their outing.

"I'd like to see where you want that first chair lift to go," Eleanor Talbot said. "You plan to make it a triple. How many skiers per hour can you lift up the mountain with that?"

Felicia was always surprised at the way this unassuming woman could interject into the conversation the most astute questions. She began to suspect that a great deal of Mr. Talbot's business success was accountable to the acumen of his wife.

After breakfast Grant went to round up the ski equipment and Felicia noticed that Ilse offered to help him.

"Me and my shadow," Nadine quipped, also taking note.

Felicia said, "My friend, let me take over the kitchen cleanup this morning. You've been so busy turning out gourmet meals, you've hardly left this room. Now get out of here."

Nadine did as she was told and left Felicia to the dishwashing. After a few minutes of soapy water and contemplation, Felicia heard Ilse come into the room.

"I've come to finish my coffee," she announced brusquely.

"You left the breakfast table in such a hurry this morning that I thought you might not be feeling well."

"I did have a bit of nausea," Ilse said with a grimace as she poured herself a cup of coffee and leaned against the old wooden drainboard where Felicia was stacking the wet dishes. "It was not the food that made me sick, it was listening to all the husband and wife stuff from Mr. and Mrs. Grant Mitchell."

"Ilse, you know why we're trying to keep the divorce a secret."

"I think it is a stupid idea."

"I don't think Grant and I have exactly been fawning on one another. We certainly didn't mean to embarrass anyone."

Ilse straightened restlessly from where she had been leaning but made no effort to find a dish towel and dry the dishes in the mountainous stack that was growing beside her.

"Grant and I," she said, repeating

Felicia's words with a nasty nasal imitation. "You make it sound like such a loving pair. But I know differently."

"What do you mean?" Felicia asked.

"I know you both went upstairs last night, pretending to head for the same room, trying to make us all think you're back in bed together. And I know it is all a big act."

"I've never tried to make you or Nadine think that. But you know very well that the Talbots are supposed to think we share a room."

"Well, I know the truth, so you don't need to portray the giggling bride around me."

"The what!" Felicia could not believe this overreaction from Ilse.

"Grant assured me beforehand that this would only be make-believe. And I just talked to him about it again. He's given me his word he didn't sleep with you last night."

"Of course he's not sleeping with me. But what business is that of yours?" Felicia struggled to restrain herself. She switched the water faucet from hot to cold, and let the stream of water cool the blood where it pumped furiously past her wrists in time to the angry thumping of her heart. When she was able to speak calmly again, she said, "Ilse, I know this whole thing is a strain on everyone. But we have to put up with it just a day or two more."

"Well, I've had enough. I won't allow it." She slammed her empty cup on the counter. "If the Talbots stay much longer, I'm going to take Grant back to Europe with me and get him away from your silly schemes."

She went out, leaving Felicia so stunned she could hardly sort out her disturbing thoughts. She could not understand why Grant would confide such intimate secrets to another woman. Why would he feel it necessary to assure Ilse that his relationship with Felicia had not been revived? Was he so involved with the woman that he must share everything with her to keep her happy and assured of his devotion to her?

As she hung up the damp towels and left the kitchen, her heart was heavy with the irony of the situation. Apparently Ilse did not realize how much Grant hated her for her lies. She didn't seem to know that Grant resented her for pretending that she had no financial worries, and for the omission she'd made when she left him without telling him she was already pregnant. And Ilse obviously wasn't aware of Grant's hatred for that shadow of the other man that would always stand between them. These things, at least, Grant had not confided in her. For if he had, Ilse would know how certain she was to be the victor in this rivalry she had set up.

Ilse was strong, self-sufficient, aggressive in going after what she wanted. While Felicia strived for these same attributes, anyone who knew her well could see through her efforts. She was no competitor. That had been her failing during her racing days, and now she had no taste for a battle with Ilse.

She went down the steps into the bleak and musty area of the basement where the atmosphere matched her mood perfectly and tried to apply herself to the furniture refinishing project she'd begun.

Five years ago Ilse had said how she felt about Grant, and Felicia had heard it. *"Je t'aime."* And now with Grant's bitterness toward Felicia at a stronger pitch than ever, it would not be long before she sensed it and turned the situation to her advantage. Without realizing at first what she was doing, Felicia crouched into the low, wind-resistant position she'd used when trying to win a skiing race. Then with a shrug she stood up. No, Ilse had nothing at all to worry about. But Felicia didn't plan to reassure her on that score.

CHAPTER NINE

The next morning after breakfast Felicia sat knitting while Eleanor Talbot relaxed in front of the fire.

"What would you like to do today?" Felicia asked her. She was looking for clues as to when they planned to leave, but she didn't want to be obvious.

"I think we'll go off on our own. I want to drive around the mountain area a bit, get a better feeling of where Deer Meadow is located in relation to the nearby highways and towns."

Again the quiet woman was analyzing, calculating, and it became obvious to Felicia that the decision about the investment would be completely in her hands. No man would discount the opinion of such a knowledgeable wife.

Grant came in, and Eleanor asked him some questions about the neighboring ski resorts. He stood with one hand resting on the back of the couch near Felicia's head, and Felicia wondered if the woman would notice how he no longer reached out to her. He was not patting her hair, or absently massaging her shoulders as he might have done that first night. But so far, amid all the strain of the people around them, the Talbots seemed blissfully unaware. They were obviously having a wonderful time.

"I think Leslie has fallen completely in love with Deer Meadow," Eleanor laughed.

Felicia looked up at Grant, and he gave her a quick return glance of relief.

"I think he pictures himself as your kindly old uncle and benefactor." Her face crinkled into a loving expression as she spoke of her husband.

Felicia could read the encouragement in Grant's face as he seemed to be counting the minutes before Mr. Talbot would hand them a check and be on his way so that he, too, could leave this place.

"Is that sweater you're knitting for your little Sally? I've seen her running around here just before her bedtime. We have no children, you know; we envy you two having a little girl. We've always been too busy with our business interests. Swim Right has been our baby. Now I think Leslie wants to help some young people get started, sort of pass on the torch. And he sees many similarities in the way you are both working together to make a nice life for your family."

Mr. Talbot came into the room then to take command of his wife, and she let him tell them all his plans for the day just as if she hadn't already made them for him. As they got into their coats and prepared to leave, Grant stood looking down at Felicia, and she wondered what he was thinking after hearing his bogus family described so admiringly. It must seem to him the ultimate insult to have to take credit for the child he thought was another man's, to have to appear proud of a wife he held in such contempt.

As soon as the Talbots had gone, Grant said, "I have a lot of paper work to see to. I'll be in my room." And he went off to leave her alone. She had hoped he might want to share with her his reactions to the good vibrations that had come from Mrs. Talbot, rejoice with her that they'd almost attained their goal.

After working all morning in the basement, Felicia was glad to take a break for lunch, and then she went into the lounge to listen to some music and wait for Sally to come home. She planned to spend the afternoon at some well-earned leisure activities. She leaned back and closed her eyes, letting the swell of Beethoven's Ninth Symphony push from her mind the morbid atmosphere created at the lunch table by Ilse's tense silence and Grant's brooding. She and Nadine had discussed their plans for menus and work schedules, ignoring the other two, but at a great cost to Felicia's tightening nerves.

"Mommy, you have your ski sweater on. Does that mean you're coming outside with me?" Sally had walked home down the short road that led from the bus stop to the lodge. Her cheeks were brightened by the cold, and Felicia looked at her with a stab of love. Moments like this served to remind her that she should not feel sorry for herself, that she had received from Grant a gift so precious that she need never ask him for more. She had his child, and that was enough.

When Grant came into the room then from the kitchen where he'd been finishing his lunch, Sally ran to him. She'd been kept so carefully occupied away from the Talbots that she'd seen very little of him in recent days, and she was blunt in letting him know she wasn't happy about it.

"Hey, coach. Will you come skiing with us? Mommy and I want you to coach us, don't we, Mommy? You haven't given me any lessons since you came here to see me."

Ilse had followed Grant out of the kitchen, and she stood watching Sally tug at Grant's hand with a bored look. "How charming," she muttered sarcastically.

She must have seen that Grant was being swayed by the child for she cut through Sally's pleadings to demand, "You must show me those budgets you've prepared, Grant. If Talbot asks you how much money is needed, you must be ready with figures."

Felicia wondered if the budget figures weren't her own responsibility, rather than Ilse's. She decided that this was the time to assert herself.

"I'd like to go over those this afternoon," she said firmly.

Grant seemed surprised, apparently realizing for the first time that Ilse had been trying to usurp her duties. The final decisions were, of course, up to Felicia.

Grant swung Sally up into his arms, cradling her in the strong steel of his hold, reminding Felicia of what it had been like to be carried through the snow by Grant when he'd come to rescue her.

"I'll tell you what," Grant said. "This little lady has fallen way behind in her training schedule. I think I'd better get out there and put her to work. And you two can go over the lists of numbers. I'm rather tired of them. I think I deserve a break."

Felicia suspected he was merely grabbing at an excuse to remove himself from the chafing spot he was in, caught between herself and Ilse.

Sally was tickling Grant behind his ear, in a spot Felicia knew to be sensitive, and he was laughing in spite of himself. She and Ilse both sat watching the two of them with equal absorption, hearing in their laughter an identical lilt, seeing carbon-copy noses lifted into the air at precisely the same angle. It was unnerving to see them together, and Felicia cast a nervous glance at Ilse, wondering if anyone else could spot the resemblance. But Ilse was too busy fuming over Grant's decision to notice anything at the moment.

Grant brought them the papers while Sally suited herself up for skiing. In a few minutes Felicia was standing at one of the windows beside the fireplace, looking out at the tall figure in black and the small figure in a tasseled red cap as they cavorted in the snow.

"You would do almost anything to get Grant back, wouldn't you, Felicia?"

"What?" Felicia turned to face Ilse who

was heaving several hefty logs into the fireplace.

"You have no conscience. Once you ran off and left him, but now you want him back and you're trying every sneaky trick to keep him here."

"You forget, Ilse, I have already lost him. We are divorced. We are no longer married."

"But you need him now, desperately. You want a husband to help run this place. You can't manage it alone."

"I'm afraid I don't agree with you on that," Felicia said, putting an overconfident sureness into her tone. "I am the sole owner of Deer Meadow, and I can oversee it just fine by myself. Grant has no intention of becoming involved in its operation. He's acting as a master planner, as he's done on countless other projects. You know that."

"Ah, yes. But you'd like to draw him into it, and draw him back into your bed as well, wouldn't you?"

"I've told you before that is none of your business," she responded hotly, determined not to let Ilse ignite her temper.

Ilse was jabbing at the logs with a poker, an almost sadistic gleam in her eye as she watched the logs catch fire and flare up. "You thought up this little game for you and Grant to play for the benefit of Mr. and Mrs. Talbot. But it was really for your benefit. You hoped Grant would forget that the husband and wife masquerade was just pretend. You planned to pull Grant back to you with memories of your glorious past together."

"None of this was my idea. Grant was the one who suggested it."

"I don't believe you. You're the one who enjoys living a lie."

"Well, I'm not lying about my plans for the future," Felicia stammered. "I had planned to come here and open a lodge with or without Grant's help. I never planned to rely on him."

Ilse was standing at the window where Felicia had been looking out, and as she watched the touching scene outside, she repeated under her breath the litany of resentment. "I know your type. You'll try anything to get your way." She turned abruptly to face Felicia. "I'll bet you're going to tell him that Sally's his own child."

Felicia was so startled that she could feel the blood draining from her face, and she knew her whitened look would tell Ilse at once that she'd made a lucky guess.

Ilse spoke louder when she continued.

"In fact, that is not a lie. He is the child's father, isn't he?"

Gripping the table beside her for support, Felicia felt disarmed to hear the sorrow of her life spoken of so openly by this woman. Ilse had thought that Felicia was going to lie about Sally's birth, pretend that Sally was Grant's own child in order to get him back. But now she'd stumbled upon the secret Felicia was trying so hard to protect.

"I'm not going to tell him that," she said, and her mind whirled in vain as she tried to think of a way to gain Ilse's silence on the matter. "Do you plan to tell him?" she finally asked with a fatalistic sigh.

"Of course not. Quite the opposite. I want him to leave here forever. I want him away from you and back in the world he enjoys, where he has good times and a successful career. Not stuck here in the Sierras with a clinging little family. I won't be the one to tell him he has a child."

Felicia was confused. Ilse seemed to see Sally as some sort of trump card in Felicia's hand. And she seemed determined not to let her play it. But why? Sally had always seemed to Felicia to be the impediment that was keeping her and Grant apart. She had never been able to believe that Grant would consider taking on the burdensome chains of a home life. He didn't want or need a home. She rubbed at her head, the turmoil inside it giving her an instant headache.

Ilse looked again through the window. "I should have known. How could I have missed it? I thought you were pushing them together, but they're drawn to each other. Father and daughter. If he ever finds out, he'll . . ."

"He'll what?" Felicia asked, not as a challenge; she sincerely wanted to know Ilse's impressions of Grant. They seemed quite different from her own.

"If he ever finds out, it will shake him up thoroughly. I don't know why you're keeping it from him. Maybe you're waiting for the exact moment," Ilse eyed her suspiciously.

"I've never told him, and I don't intend to do so now," she said. She knew she could not tell him. Once she had considered it in a rash moment, but she had put that idea aside forever when he'd called her an unfaithful wife, when she'd seen that he could believe her child had been born of a man she never even married. He was too rigid in his thinking to ever erase those first blemished impressions of Sally.

She had been filled with panic just a

moment before, thinking that Ilse would tell him about Sally. But now she realized that they both wanted the same thing: to protect Grant from the truth so that he could pursue without guilt the life he needed to live.

As the two women stood facing one another, their faces filled with signs of furious mental activity as they assessed one another's motives, Eleanor and Leslie Talbot came in the front door. They must have guessed at once that they'd interrupted a quarrel, because they began throwing off their coats in a hurry to get to their rooms and not intrude. But Felicia went to the coatrack near them and pulled her parka off a hook.

"I'm going for a walk until dinner. Ilse, tell Nadine to give Sally her bath. You can manage dinner, can't you?"

"Of course," Ilse said tersely.

Eleanor Talbot seemed anxious to be of help in soothing the situation. "I'll be glad to help out. I think I can still peel a potato."

For once Felicia didn't care how things got done. She went out the front door and down the road that led through the trees toward the main road. She tried to admire the beauty of the late afternoon slant of sun on snow, the pink and gold glow that the sunset had painted upon the white fields. But always her thoughts came back to Grant.

Ilse thought Grant would stay here if he knew Sally was his own; she was afraid he would want to make a home with a wife and child. But Felicia had never been able to picture him making such a choice. Did Ilse see him as a man of principle who would recognize his duty to the child he had fathered? Felicia couldn't bear to think of Grant tied down to a dreary responsibility just because he thought he must fulfill obligations and do the right thing — without any sense of love. Or did Ilse recognize a mellowing, a maturing in Grant, that would make him appreciate such homey values as hearth and home? Had he changed in the years since she'd known him? Or maybe he had even had such nurturing tendencies five years ago and she'd been too young and impatient to find them.

No, that was impossible. He'd never once spoken of having a family. All he had wanted was for her to keep collecting those downhill medals. All he had wanted was to keep the good times coming.

After the sun set, the evening became bitter with cold, but she walked on, lost in her disturbing new thoughts. She felt a nasty chill shake her, and she wrapped the parka closer to her body with her arms around herself.

I've changed a lot in the years since Sally was born. She's changed me, softened me, and given me an eye for the tiny moments of joy in the world. I've learned to sew and knit and listen to music and fix furniture and find pleasure in all of those things. As I've matured, my goals have changed. I don't demand so much excitement out of life. Has Grant changed? Have the years softened him any?

At last she turned back and began walking toward the lodge again. She walked faster, anxious to be in out of the icy weather. She was glad she'd taken the walk, her headache was gone and her thoughts were more orderly now, coming at a pace she could deal with. But she felt frozen to the bone, and in need of some time to thaw before the fire.

As soon as she came into the lodge, she realized there was no time for that. Nadine was putting Sally to bed, but Felicia had to go upstairs to give her the final tuck-in. Then Nadine informed her that Eleanor was working in the kitchen all alone, so they both hurried downstairs to help her get dinner together. As she passed through the lounge, she noticed that Ilse was huddled near the fire in intense conversation with Grant. Felicia paused a moment, wondering what they were talking about, but since Grant didn't look her way, she felt confident that it was a business matter.

Tomorrow she was going to sit with Grant and talk. She was going to ask him what he wanted out of life. She was going to learn more about his hopes and dreams, what his ideal future would be. Why hadn't she already done that? This was a man she'd been married to and supposedly known intimately. This was someone she'd just realized she was still in love with. But his enigmatic barrier of strength had defied her penetration. She had never dared to try to pierce his reserve and look for the inner man.

"My dear, I hope you haven't caught cold. Your lips are blue!" Eleanor admonished her, apparently enjoying playing the mother hen of Deer Meadow.

"I'm fine. I'll warm up in a minute if I keep busy," Felicia shivered.

During dinner Ilse was again her old self, keeping everyone else out of the conversation with her long descriptions of the lodges she'd managed in the Harz Mountains and the Black Forest. "How would you compare Davos to Zermatt, Grant?"

she asked, taking on Switzerland after she'd thoroughly covered the German resorts. The only one she seemed interested in drawing into the conversation was Grant, and she was making an obvious attempt to remind him of the exotic pleasure spots he must be missing.

"You've always loved Saint Moritz, haven't you?" she asked. "And isn't Engelberg becoming more popular again?"

Everyone else concentrated on the meal, until Leslie Talbot finally found an opening.

"I've decided you're quite right about cross-country skiing, Grant. It's becoming more popular, and I think you could offer an excellent program here. Before we leave, I'd like to take a look at that spot you suggested for a wilderness base camp."

"When do you think you'll be leaving?" Ilse asked rudely, without regard for good manners.

"Oh, I think we'll stay till the weekend. That's what Eleanor suggested," Talbot said.

Ilse was giving Grant a stern look that just might have been accompanied by a kick on the shins under the table.

"I'm sorry I won't be able to stay and take you touring," Grant said. "I have some deals brewing in Europe that I must see to."

Now Felicia understood what Ilse had been priming Grant for. She wanted him away from here as soon as possible.

"Do you have to go, darling?" she asked sweetly, enjoying Ilse's sultry jealousy and Grant's lifted eyebrow.

"I'm leaving right after dinner, actually. I thought I'd drive to L.A. tonight and catch a direct flight to Europe tomorrow morning."

Felicia's heart thudded down to her after-ski boots, in spite of her pretense of cheerful acceptance. "I guess we'll have to get along without you for a little while," she smiled at him. He gave her a questioning smile in return, his senses alerted as he tried to guess her real reaction.

Now that she knew he was leaving, and probably for good, she feasted her eyes upon him, knowing that she could do it freely in the name of wifely devotion, maintaining the pose. She let her eyes rove over him, stopping to study the rugged outdoor glow that dusted his high cheekbones with color, lingering briefly at the dark eyes with their piercing flare of interest. She took in the abundant dark mop of hair that hung shaggy over his brow, and then came to rest on the mouth she would never feel against hers again.

As the others at the table talked on, confirming plans for the rest of the week, she said her farewell to the provocative lips that she wished she could touch with her fingertips. But instead she used her eyes, reaching out to touch him with her look, feeling a melting within her that brought hotness to her cheeks.

Grant's composure had obviously been shaken by the intensity of her scan. His tongue quickly swiped across his lips, and he put down his fork to discontinue any attempt at eating. She could tell from the vibrations of his muscular chest beneath his sweater that he was breathing hard, and she fervently wished she had more powerful weapons to use, a way to make him change his mind and stay. But when Nadine got up to serve dessert, he made his apologies and got up from the table to go pack, his eyes only leaving Felicia's when she gave up, conceded the struggle, and looked back down at her plate. She blinked back tears, and Eleanor, sitting beside her, noticed and reached over to pat her hand.

"Now, Felicia. Don't let this upset you. He'll be back soon."

No he won't. He'll never come back. He's lost to me for good.

An hour later Grant came down the stairs into the lounge with two suitcases, and the Talbots went to the door to bid him off. Felicia followed hesitantly behind, her face feeling drawn tight with discouragement, wondering if she would get a moment alone with him.

Eleanor Talbot leaned her cheek toward Grant, offering it for a kiss. "I feel as if we've known you forever, you and your sweet wife. We haven't had much opportunity to get to know your daughter, but she seems a darling little girl." She reached up to pat her gray hair, looking for something to say to please him before he left on his long journey. "Sally looks like her mother, but she certainly has her father's eyes."

Felicia's eyelashes fluttered as she looked up at Grant, dreading his reply.

"I suppose she probably does have her father's eyes. I wonder if she inherited his powers of persuasion as well."

He looked at Felicia, reminding her that he still believed Sally's father had won Felicia away from him.

"Well, you've persuaded us, young man," Leslie Talbot said, shaking Grant's hand. "We're sold on this project. My banker will be in touch with you."

Just then they all turned at the sound of

baggage thumping onto the floor behind them. Ilse was standing between the suitcases she had carried from her room, dressed for travel in a long gray cape with the hood thrown back to frame her victorious facial expression.

"You're going too?" Felicia blurted out.

"Your husband has very kindly consented to give me a ride to the airport. I must get back and catch up on my work. I've neglected my job there for too long."

Nadine called out to her from across the room. "Good-bye, Ilse. Thanks for all your help," with a sound like a cheer after her team's winning touchdown. She had been counting the hours until Ilse and her sententious advice were gone.

While Felicia was glad to be rid of her, she could not feel the same exultant relief. Though Ilse had been careful to imply otherwise in her public comments, Felicia was certain that she was going with Grant, taking him wherever she might be headed, whisking him far from any lingering instinct that might lure him to remain with Felicia. Just as Felicia had predicted, Grant had grown restless after a couple of weeks in one place. He was itching to be on the move again, and Ilse had known just how to fester that itch.

Ilse picked up her suitcases again, with no visible strain to her broad shoulders, and walked out the door. Grant was following her, and Mr. Talbot seemed to be preparing to walk with him right on out to the porch.

"Leslie, give them a moment alone together," Eleanor whispered to her husband, stopping him with a gentle hand on his arm. She gave Felicia a nod of encouragement that sent her hurrying to take Leslie Talbot's place.

The porch was cold and dark, but Felicia didn't need to see to feel Grant's eyes on her. Hearing her come out and close the door behind her, he had stopped at the steps and turned to face her. He seemed reluctant to leave yet. Felicia suspected from his tensely coiled stance that there were charges he still wanted to make against her, hurts he still needed to repay her for.

To erase the silence, she uttered any inanity she could think of. "Thank you for coming to help, Grant."

When he didn't answer her, she went on. "I know it's hard for you to be in one place for very long. I appreciate how long you've stayed." She curled her cold fingers nervously into fists.

"I really haven't minded," he said more

pleasantly than she had expected. "You've made this a hard place to leave. That's why the Talbots have been so impressed. You've made this old wreck seem like a home. You'll be a big success running this lodge, Felicia, have no doubts."

"It's hard for you to leave, but you must?"

Felicia was crying out for him to stay, but her words were too mild to convey the message. Behind him she could hear the heavy noises of Ilse dropping her suitcases into the trunk of the car.

"The atmosphere here is seducing. And that look you gave me at the dinner table, if you give that to every guest who threatens to check out, you'll never have an empty room." When she didn't laugh at his joke, he continued. "Even when I know you're faking, you have a powerful effect on me, Felicia."

He put down the suitcases to step closer to where she was standing at the door. As he came toward her, she felt a tingling that started at the top of her head and moved slowly downward, with a cascading effect of mounting tension. Tiny pinpricks of pain and pleasure moved down her face and neck in a shower. He came close enough to touch her, and as he reached out to take her shoulders in his hands, the feeling that had been building in her head exploded. She sneezed once, then again. He tightened his hands, absorbing the shock as her body convulsed each time.

"Grant, time to go!" Ilse called out to him from the darkness.

He never loosened his grasp on Felicia's shoulders. "Wait," he commanded with all the imperious force that was required in dealing with Ilse. "Wait," he whispered huskily to Felicia, standing motionless holding her.

She felt a suspension of all time: an oscillating silence filled the void in the air with waiting. She lifted her head in anticipation, stretching her graceful neck away from the long straight curtain of light hair that surrounded it. Then she sneezed again.

"You see. I know you always sneeze in threes. I was waiting for that last one."

Felicia's eyes felt moist with disappointment. The sneezes had shaken some of the nervous rigidity from her body, but she knew now that the real relief she had hoped for in Grant's arms was not going to be offered.

Grant ran his hands down her sleeves, squeezing just enough to bring a ripple of response following his fingers. "You're cold. You'd better get inside."

Just as she turned to pull from him with all her hopes dashed, he leaned down suddenly to kiss her cheek, and he reared back with such a quick movement that she wondered if he had tasted the salty tears that were spilled there.

"We must be on our way, Grant." Ilse had come back up the front walk to recapture him. Seeing that only Felicia was there to catch her point, she said, "They won't hold our reservation at that airport hotel forever."

As the car drove away, she stood watching the red taillights disappear into the darkness and wondered if she had again avoided a conflict, withdrawn before the race was over. Her opponent, Ilse, had accused her of using every method she could to keep Grant here, but had she put her heart into any real try? Consciously she hadn't planned any campaign. Until the very last moment she had believed it was futile to dream of recapturing their early days of bliss, when so much had happened since to shut her out of the competition. But, she thought, if she hadn't hoped for something better, why did she feel so defeated and alone now that he was gone forever?

CHAPTER TEN

Felicia came back into the lodge, clapping her hands in front of her and behind her back alternately with long swings of her arms as she tried to appear undaunted.

"Now listen everyone, the manager has an announcement to make."

Nadine and the Talbots looked up from the jigsaw puzzle they were assembling on a card table.

Felicia went on forcing her purposefulness through tight teeth. "Nadine, as of this moment I'm taking over your kitchen duties. You haven't taken a day off since we got here. I want you to take my car and go do something different. Shop for that kitchen equipment in Bishop if you want; just get away from here for a few days."

It was Felicia who needed to get away, who craved a means of escape from the lingering aura of Grant that pervaded the place, but Nadine didn't recognize the distorted reasoning going on in Felicia's mind.

"Warden, thank you for setting me free," she said to show her agreement.

Felicia hoped that taking on Nadine's chores would keep her too busy to think. However, the next day, after Nadine had gone, she found she'd gotten more activity than she bargained for. Sally complained of a sore throat and stayed home from school in bed. Felicia ran from the cold basement, where her furniture project was, up to the second-floor sickroom which was kept warm and cozy for her patient. Then she'd stop off in the kitchen to stuff a chicken or put a pie in the hot oven, and it was back upstairs with a pitcher of orange juice. The Talbots didn't require much care, but there were towels to gather up and beds to change while they were out. Felicia was determined not to make them feel they were getting second-class service now that the staff had been reduced to one.

At dinner that night she expended every last ounce of her energy in an attempt to seem gay and friendly. She didn't want to show her fatigue and make Leslie and Eleanor feel unwelcome. But as soon as she had eaten, she said, "If you'll excuse me, I think I'll clean up and then get to bed early."

On Saturday Sally was feeling much better and consequently was in need of almost constant amusement. As Felicia headed to her room with a coloring book in one hand

and an aspirin bottle in the other, Mrs. Talbot stopped her with a worried look.

"Slow down, Felicia, or you'll be the next one sick in bed. Your face is gray and there are black circles under your eyes. I never thought I'd see such a beautiful girl wear herself down like this." The wrinkles under her own eyes doubled in evidence of her concern.

"I'm all right. A mother always worries over a child with a cold."

"Well, I'm worried about you. Let me take those up. Maybe I can read to Sally for a while."

"No, no! I have to go up anyway to check on something." She didn't need the extra concern of wondering when Eleanor would bring up the subject of "Daddy" with Sally.

"I have an idea, then," Eleanor said, refusing to give up. "Let me cook our farewell dinner tonight."

"Farewell?"

"Yes, we're going to leave early tomorrow morning. We love it here, but we have neglected the business world long enough."

Felicia knew from watching the older woman's last attempt at help in the kitchen that she was not a very practiced cook, but she was in no position to ignore the offer of help.

"I'll run down to the store and buy some steaks," she said, thinking out loud. "That will be a good celebration." She felt sure she could prompt Eleanor through the simple preparations for steak, baked potatoes, and tossed salad between her trips up to Sally.

The two of them did get the meal on the table, just as planned and right on time. Felicia opened a bottle of vintage Pinot Noir from the cases Grant had chosen to stock their wine cupboard and Leslie offered the first toast.

"To our hostess, with her sparkling eyes, and her cheeks like roses in the snow. Thank you for making us feel at home here."

Eleanor tasted the wine, then regarded Felicia carefully. "Her eyes are sparkling just a bit too brightly, and her cheeks are pink because they're warm."

"My words were more romantic," her husband grumbled.

"I don't think Felicia feels very romantic with her husband so far away," Eleanor said. "You haven't complained once, Felicia, but I can see how much you depend on him. From the moment he left, there has been a lost look on your face."

Felicia felt sick with herself for the way she had deceived this woman. "Eleanor, I wish I could speak frankly to you before you leave. I must confess something. I hope you can forgive me . . ." Felicia stumbled, realizing her words were coming out in a jumble, but her mind was oddly hazy tonight, and she couldn't think of how to explain herself.

"In the years ahead I think we'll become good friends, and then you can tell me anything. I can see you have problems on your mind, even though you've worked so hard to hide them. They are problems that our financial investment here won't alleviate. But for what it's worth, you are going to have your capital for the improvements you've planned. And I hope that news will cheer you."

"Oh, Eleanor, Leslie, it's your advice and your presence here that I want, most of all. Even if you don't invest in Deer Meadow, promise you'll come here often."

"Didn't I tell your husband that my banker would be calling?" Leslie said. "The money will be on its way before you know it."

"And we'll be on our way for another visit very soon," Eleanor added.

Felicia was so overcome by her thankful feelings that she had to mumble an apology and leave the table. She stood in one of the dark shadows of the kitchen, wiping at her eyes and blowing her nose.

She was not going to be entirely alone! She would have surrogate parents to guide her. Even if they did live far away and their visits were sporadic, maybe she could call on them for support if ever she should falter. She tried to control her tears, but it felt good to let them flow, to wash herself free of that fear of abandonment which plagued her.

Her own father had disappeared from her life before she ever knew him. Her mother had divorced him when she and her brother were very small. Using her alimony, Felicia's mother had then embarked on a lifetime of enjoying herself, moving from one glamour city to another. She was as dependable as a butterfly, selfish and unloving. Felicia's brother had gone away to college and then marriage and a career, so that he rarely came into her life except to handle a legal matter like the divorce. And then there had been Grant, the one she'd hoped would be the rock-solid foundation she could build her life upon. But that underfooting had collapsed beneath her feet. And his recent departure had underscored her feelings of being deserted.

Now Mr. and Mrs. Talbot had promised

her that the future of Deer Meadow was secure. And she was imagining they would extend that commitment to cover her own future as well, both physical and emotional. She knew she was grasping at them, expecting too much, but like the sobs it felt good.

Leslie at last came to drag her back to the table. "We expected you to be happy, but we didn't expect this big a show. Why, your own husband could probably put twice as much money into this project as we're going to, and never miss it."

"But your investment is a real show of faith," she sniffed. "Now I know I was right to stay here, to believe in it." Seeing Eleanor's attentive look, she corrected herself. "I mean, Grant and I were right to believe in it."

The next morning her alarm clock rang and rang before she could finally shake herself awake to turn it off. She was determined to get up and see the Talbots off with hot coffee. The effort of slipping into a robe seemed tiring, so she knew the night's sleep had done little to replenish her dwindling strength. She padded down the stairs in her warm shearling slippers, gripping the handrail to steady herself, her head still dizzy with sleepiness.

She was almost relieved to find a note saying her guests had gotten an early start and were already gone. She stumbled back upstairs, lifting each foot as if she were dragging ski boots. Finding Sally still asleep, and realizing the two of them were alone here, that she had no others to make demands on her, she went back into her room and fell into bed.

But with the free time to let her mind be creative, she couldn't help but wonder where Grant was now, what he was doing, who he was with. But, of course, he would be with Ilse. Today he would be riding the Nebelhornbahn cable-car lift, skiing at Herzogenhorn, or drinking beer from frosty steins with Ilse. And tonight? What would he be doing tonight? She turned her pillow over, then sank her face against the cool side.

Felicia knew that beneath the brusque veneer, Ilse was a deeply passionate woman. She'd taken the full brunt of Ilse's jealousy and anger and found her emotions to be larger than life. She couldn't help but imagine that Ilse was equally passion-filled when she was alone with Grant, but on a more physical level. She would doubtless aim all her ardor at pleasing him, making love to him, helping him forget the long dull weeks in the Sierras.

When the hideous visions of Ilse and Grant together became too much for her, she got up and dressed, and hearing Sally's call, went to take care of her. She worked the rest of the morning as if in a frenzy, cleaning rooms that didn't need it, scrubbing floors that already gleamed. When Nadine returned, Felicia was in the kitchen, trying to lift a heavy lunch tray to take to Sally, but the thing felt as if it were nailed to the counter.

"My God, Felicia, what are you doing?"

Felicia tried to answer her, but only a croaking sound came from her constricted throat.

"You look awful. You're sick and you belong in bed. Something told me I should get back here early today." Nadine gave her friend a worried look as she watched how obediently Felicia shuffled from the room.

Felicia spent the rest of the day sleeping, awakening only once when a racking cough shook her like a rag doll. Nadine came in then with some soup, but she could barely swallow, and the effort of sitting up was too great, so Nadine shook her head with discouragement and left the room.

The next day passed fitfully for her, with

sleep and coughing again taking turns controlling her. Her bones ached, and when she tried to get up, they would barely support her body. She made her way toward the bathroom, grabbing furniture as she went to steady her shaky legs. She splashed water on her face to cool it, then looked into the mirror and drew back with a gasp. Her hair was matted and tangled around a white face that seemed frightening in its lifelessness. Her eyes burned like blue pilot lights, bright but giving off no radiating reflection. On her way back to bed she fell across the rocker in a near faint, and Nadine came in to find her there.

"This isn't just a cold. You have a full-scale flu. Now get back into that bed," Nadine pronounced sternly. "Sally's gone back to school today, and you have nothing to worry about but getting well."

"But those men are coming to put in the carpet Ilse ordered for the halls. I must . . ."

"You must sleep," Nadine said, drawing the curtains and leaving her with a door closed so that nothing would disturb her.

But her own mind was the cause of most of her disturbance. It fought her body, insisting it get up and see to running the place. She felt she must prove that she could manage things without Grant here.

In the years ahead this lodge would be her sole responsibility and her livelihood. She couldn't afford to rest, didn't dare trust anyone else to make decisions. The weight was hers alone to carry. But her shaking, sweating shoulders were too weak to lift the burden that day, or the next, no matter how hard she tried to push herself.

She was aware of the day passing, of Sally's intermittent visits, with her brown eyes wide and worried, and of Nadine's bustling attempts to comfort her with hot lemon juice and honey, or fresh sheets on her bed.

One night was a particular horror, with dreams that terrified her so that she called out for Grant to come again and save her. But this time she was lost in a hot desert, her skin parched and burning under a relentless sun.

"Grant, please find me. Grant, please come."

"He's coming, Felicia. I've called him."

"What?" She sat up in bed, but Nadine pushed her back onto the wadded mass of pillows.

"I found the number of that New York office on your notepad. They just called me back; they've located him and given him the message to come."

"Oh, Nadine, you shouldn't have done that. I don't want him to feel he has to help me. He mustn't come back just because I can't make it alone."

"You've called out for him every night in your sleep. I don't think you'll ever get well without him."

Felicia fell back, exhausted by the strain of her argument. She plummeted immediately into a feverish sleep that seemed to go on for an eternity.

When next she opened her eyes, it was in response to someone opening her door, sending a slice of light across her bed. She knew from the size of the massive form filling her doorway that it was Grant. He was breathing fast, apparently having run up the stairs. She could see he hadn't stopped to unwind the knitted muffler that was wrapped around his neck over his tweed sportcoat.

He came to the side of her bed and turned on the light. The sight of him was potent medicine, and she blinked rapidly to bring him into focus. He looked too rugged, his face still tinged with the healthy look of outdoors, to be visiting a sickroom. There was a coating of new-fallen snow graying his dark hair that made her aware of the outside world for the first time in days.

"Grant, you didn't have to come. I'll be up and taking care of things tomorrow." Her words came slowly, forced between the efforts of her congested lungs to draw in air.

He leaned down and gently pulled the blond hair apart where it covered her forehead and kissed her on the warm skin he'd exposed. His voice was as soft as a falling flake of snow when he spoke.

"I don't mind being needed. It felt kind of nice to be summoned back home to look after someone."

Felicia reached her hand out to him, vulnerable in her weakened condition. "I am glad you're here," she whispered.

She realized that others had come into the room, and Grant was speaking to them with more urgency than he'd shown to her.

"What's her temperature, Nadine? She seems very hot."

"It was just over a hundred and one the last time I checked."

"She's hot because she's been bedded down in this stuffy room, that's all."

Felicia recognized Ilse's voice and rolled over onto her side with a loud groan, too ill to conceal her despair at finding Grant had brought her back with him.

"Go downstairs, Ilse," he told her. "I

agreed to let you come to help, not to upset people."

When they were again alone together, Grant pulled a chair up beside the bed.

"I'm sorry you had to leave what you were doing in Europe," she said tentatively, meaning his travels with Ilse.

"My business there is complete," he said.

"What do you mean, complete?"

"I've set things in motion, signed all the necessary papers. My agents can handle the rest."

"What are you doing?" her voice sounded scratchy, and he offered her a glass of water, putting his arm behind her pillow to lift her toward it.

"I'm selling off everything I own over there. I've decided that I want to settle in one place now. I'm ready to devote myself to one project, making this lodge a skiing showplace."

"Here? You're going to settle here?" The heavy weight of her illness, which had seemed to be crushing her chest until now, lifted slightly.

"You made me realize what a home can be. I found that I didn't ever want to leave here again."

Felicia rubbed at her face, trying to clear away the hazy blur before her eyes that was obliterating his meaning.

"But I don't understand why you want to be here." Did he mean he loved her; did he want to be her husband again?

Grant's eyes suddenly turned flinty, the way she was more used to seeing them.

"I realize you might prefer someone else as a partner. But, Felicia, he's never treated you right. He's never been there when you needed him. And you need someone now."

"Someone else? Who are you talking about?"

"Sally's father. I know how you still feel about him. You won't allow anything said against him, you protect him in spite of what he's done to you."

Grant's voice showed some of the pain he still felt, and with a sickening surge of empathy she realized how long he had carried that scar. She had to tell him now, let him know she hadn't left him for another man, hadn't had a child by another man. There was no other man. She'd always loved him.

Her mouth flew open to gasp for air, and she was so excited by her intentions to heal the painful rent in his heart that she choked and began to cough.

"You rest now. Try to sleep. You're too sick to worry about the future. We'll work everything out later." His hands were warm and strong as they held her down.

"Don't leave."

"Shh. I'll sit right here."

Her breathing was labored, but it gradually slowed, and she tried to sleep and lose herself in the dreams he was offering her.

She had misjudged him. He wanted a stable life, a house with a child in it. He wanted to work at a family business and build for the future. They could be together again and for always. But it tortured her to think that Ilse had been right, that she could have told him about Sally and had him back.

She rolled about restlessly on the bed, feeling the sheets beneath her dampen with her perspiration. How would he feel now, learning that she had kept him from this family life with her wild stories? He might be angry, thinking of the wasted years he could have shared with his daughter. Felicia's youthful insecurity had pushed him out of their lives. Now she could imagine his wrathful indignation when he learned what she'd deprived him of.

None of this was his fault. I doubted him. I never offered him the choice. He detested those other lies, and when he finds out Sally's his child, he'll turn against me forever. He'll hate me for never giving him a chance.

She clawed at the sheets that covered her, clenching them into wads in her hot hands. Grant was not like her mother; he was unique, and complicated. And she had denied him the right to prove he could grow and change.

"Here! Put this thermometer under your tongue."

Grant was leaning over her, one hand on her forehead. His face seemed tired, the craggy lines deeper around his mouth.

"Grant, you have to understand. I didn't think you loved me enough to change for me." She threw off the confining covers which she'd twisted into a tangle around herself.

"Quiet now. Keep your mouth closed."

"I did it because I couldn't bear to have you resent her the rest of our lives."

He gave the blue comforter a swift snap in the air, then recovered her with it, tucking it around her chin with a grave gesture of finality. Then he stood as straight as a ski beside her bed, watching her, his legs planted so firmly that she could see the muscles of his thighs tighten beneath the dark fabric of his pant legs. To her near-delirious mind, he seemed forbidding, a severe taskmaster guarding her.

And she was sure that his strictness went deeper. His code of ethics was rigid and unyielding. His revenge on her would be pitiless when he learned what she'd robbed him of.

She sat up, pulling the thermometer from her mouth and throwing it down on the quilt.

"Oh, Grant. You're going to hate me," she cried out.

She leaned out of the bed and grabbed onto him, wrapping her arms around one of his strong legs, burying her face against his hip, rubbing her face to and fro against the harsh fabric there, burrowing and pleading incoherently.

"You'll never be able to forgive me. I know you'll never understand why I did it. But please don't leave me again."

He brushed his hand across her hair to still her, but he wasn't listening to her.

"Nadine, come here!" he was calling, raising his voice with a stridency that had a trace of a tremor in it. "Go get me her coat and some boots."

"What's wrong?" Nadine came rushing from her room next door, tying a robe around herself.

"I'm taking her to a hospital. We'll never get a doctor to come way out here in a snowstorm. I think her temperature just shot through the roof."

He sat beside her on the bed to button her into her warm clothing while she floundered limply against him. He pulled her crocheted cap over her hair and rolled the edges up neatly around her face, stopping then to lay his hands flat on each of her cheeks. With his thumbs he lightly stroked her cheekbones as she stared at him with glazed and tormented eyes. She could tell he was worried about her, but her own concerns were deeper. She knew her secret had come back to threaten her life in new and more terminal ways.

"I'll be right back, Felicia. Do you hear me? I'm going to go start up the car and get the heater running."

The slam of the front door must have awakened Ilse downstairs, for in just a moment she came flying into Felicia's room, her hair loose and flying about her angry face.

"What are you up to now? First you bring him all the way back to this outpost as if it were some emergency, and now you're dragging him out in a snowstorm. How can he believe this? He must be able to see that you're faking, trying anything to win his sympathy!" Her voice was guttural, the words spit out in a torrent. Felicia could only look dumbly back at her, feeling a mounting hatred for the desperately combatant woman.

Grant brushed past Ilse, too concerned with his objective to have heard her tirade. He wrapped the quilt around Felicia and then lifted her into his arms. But at the doorway Ilse stood defiantly blocking their way.

"Why do you care what happens to her? She's kept from you the one thing you've always wanted. She's made a fool of you. She's never even told you that the child is yours. Sally's your daughter."

Grant slowly lowered his arms, letting Felicia's feet drop to the floor until she was standing in a trembling heap in front of him. There was a deathly silence in the room, and Felicia gathered the quilt around her shoulders, feeling her fury strengthen her.

"When I get back from the hospital, Ilse, *if* I ever get back from the hospital, I want you gone," Felicia shouted, being overly dramatic and not minding a bit. "You are a ruthless, cruel, overbearing woman, and I never want to see you at Deer Meadow again. You two-bit Valkyrie! You cold, in-human . . ."

"Stop! That's enough, Felicia. You'll wear yourself out." Grant picked her up again with a swift lurch that frightened her and stomped off down the stairs, jostling her cruelly. He dumped her into the car, and then went to the driver's side and drove off, his hands taut and white-knuckled on the steering wheel. Felicia huddled against the door on her side of the car, wishing she could cry or scream to release her agony.

Their car slid and bumped over the snowy roads, but Grant seemed to disregard all the hazards and drove recklessly through the dark snowfall, saying nothing. She could tell he was preoccupied, caring less about their safety than about the news Ilse had blurted out to him. They passed quickly through the darkened settlement at Buckskin Village and turned onto the main highway that would take them to the hospital in Clarita Valley.

Up ahead Felicia noticed flashing yellow lights, and Grant muttered an oath as soon as he saw that it was a huge snowplow that they could not get past. He jammed on the brakes, and the car went into a long skid, veering across the road and into the high roadside snow.

"Oh, great. I wonder how long we'll be stuck here?" he muttered under his breath.

"Maybe the next snowplow will pull us loose."

He looked over at her, his eyes so dead they seemed to be beyond hope of revival. "Stay bundled up. I'll keep the engine running so the heater will keep you warm. I guess you're no worse off here than you would be at home in bed."

"Will you let me talk to you? Will you listen if I tell you how it all happened? Will you try to understand?"

"You're as full of questions as your daughter," he said with a twisted smile. "As our daughter." The words froze on his lips, and his face registered all his internal questions as he tried the idea on for size. "Our daughter?"

"Yes, she's ours."

He lowered his head so that his thick lashes made his expression unreadable. "Then there never was any other man?"

"No, he was just a phantom."

"But why did you ever invent him?"

"I had to think of a way to leave you before you found out I was pregnant. And I didn't want you to follow me and try to change my mind. I thought you wouldn't want a child. I knew you liked that foot-loose life, dashing from city to city, flirting with all the girls."

"There was never any other woman for me but my wife."

"You knew Ilse then," she said haltingly. "I heard her on the phone with you once, telling you she loved you."

"Now that you've met her, you must know that she's the type who will say most anything," he said with a hollow laugh that seemed to dismiss her as of no importance in his life.

"I was young, I guess I made a lot of mistakes," Felicia admitted. "I should have trusted you. I should have let you decide. Maybe you could have adjusted to the idea of becoming a father."

"I don't honestly know what I would have done," he said, quietly appraising himself.

"You mean, things might have turned out just the same?" she asked, feeling that tightness in her throat again.

"You may have been right about the kind of man I was then. I didn't think much about what I wanted out of life. I don't think I even knew until you left how much I loved you." He was looking straight ahead of him, watching the snow fall on the windshield, but then he turned his entire body sideways on the seat to face her. "I don't want you ever to feel guilty over what you did. You wanted our child, and you were protecting her before she was even born. And maybe you knew me too well. Maybe I wasn't ready then." He leaned over to fumble through the coverings over her and find her hand. "But I'm ready now."

Felicia allowed some optimism to illuminate her darkest recesses. She caught her breath, her face transparent as it revealed the hope that enlivened it. "You're ready to claim your family?"

"Yes," he said gravely. "And I'll make it up to Sally for the lost years. I may be a pretty uneducated father at first, but I'm going to love learning about it."

He pushed himself across the seat toward her, pressing so heavily against her that she was crushed into the door. He lowered his head to nuzzle her hair with his lips.

"I have a lot to make up to you, too. I'm going to make you a wealthy woman, the envy of the ski world." He paused to kiss her cheek. "I'm also going to make you a happy wife again. I love you, Felicia. And I'll always cherish our days together, knowing what it's like to lose you."

She looked up at him, smiling her love into his face.

"If I try to kiss you, are you going to

sneeze again and spoil things?" he asked.

"No way! I'm cured."

He took her into his arms to kiss her.

It was a husbandly kiss, with none of the anger or bitterness to it that had impeded them before. It was full of provocative promises of the many long nights of fulfillment that were ahead of them. She reached up to twine her fingers through his silky black hair, and her lips fell open to him, welcoming the warmth of his tongue, the tender ministrations of his caring.

"Hey, buddy, you want me to tow you, or are you happy where you are?" A harsh voice was calling to them through the steam-frosted windows of the car.

Grant jumped back behind the wheel with a throaty chuckle, and soon they were on their way back down the highway.

At the hospital Grant led her by the hand to the emergency room physician, and waited with her while her temperature and blood pressure were taken. He couldn't seem to take his eyes off of her, and he hovered over the young doctor, asking questions.

"You say her temperature is normal? But I think it was quite high just a short while ago."

"That can happen. She looks fine to me

now. The crisis seems to have passed. She's just had a rather nasty case of the flu. It's going around."

The doctor left the curtained cubicle to get her the medication he'd prescribed. Grant stepped over a white stool and sat down, looking at her as if her restored health was a miracle.

"I think that outburst of temper you unleashed on Ilse burned off your fever."

"I'm not going to do that any more," she promised. "No more tantrums. No more name-calling."

"I don't want you to teach my Sally bad habits," he said, his smile melting away her every bad memory of the past.

She reached out to touch his face. "How good it sounds to hear you call her that. And it sounds so natural. You are different now. There's a gentleness to you that I am going to have to learn about." His transformation made him seem to her even more of a man than he'd ever been.

"I've changed, and so have you," he said. "Our love is going to be fresh and new, like two people coming together for the first time, as adults, as completed people."

She caressed the tight skin that covered his cheekbones, confident that she would be sheltered and defended by his dependable presence from now on, her reward for waiting for him.

"We're going to have more children, a big brood to keep Deer Meadow humming," he said. "I want to see them when they're young, and I want to be there for them when they need me." He paused thoughtfully. "But Sally will always be special. She's the reminder of that young love we shared which we must never deny or forget. It was careless and free and irresponsible and it brought us a lot of heartache, but it was glorious, too, and we're going to keep it with us."

The doctor came in and handed Felicia a small bottle. "I think you'll be fine," he said and left.

She looked at Grant with shining eyes. "I think he's right. I'll be just fine from now on."

Grant's face was full of resolution, offering her a future with him that was secure, a love that was inseparable. He held out his hand to her. "Let's go home."

Her heart slid downhill at a racer's speed to the place where it belonged, into the palm of Grant's hand.

We hope you have enjoyed this Large Print book. Other Thorndike, Wheeler or Chivers Press Large Print books are available at your library or directly from the publishers.

For more information about current and up-coming titles, please call or write, without obligation, to:

Publisher
Thorndike Press
295 Kennedy Memorial Drive
Waterville, ME   04901
Tel. (800) 223-1244

Or visit our Web site at:
www.gale.com/thorndike
www.gale.com/wheeler

OR

Chivers Large Print
published by BBC Audiobooks Ltd
St James House, The Square
Lower Bristol Road
Bath BA2 3SB
England
Tel. +44(0) 800 136919
email: bbcaudiobooks@bbc.co.uk
www.bbcaudiobooks.co.uk

All our Large Print titles are designed for easy reading, and all our books are made to last.